Gosh Darn Griffins

Book Two of Magic and Motherhood

A. L. Tippett

Ebook ISBN: 978-0-6455730-6-0

Paperback ISBN: 978-0-6455730-7-7

Cover designed by Ravenborn Covers

Chapter art designed by Urban Rex Designs

Published by FireFly Books

Australian spelling and grammar used throughout this book.

FIRE FLY
BOOKS

Contents

Author's Note

Dear reader,

Just a friendly PSA: this series is based in Australia, and guess what? There are Australians in Australia. Many of us are foul-mouthed and use Aussie slang on a daily basis and this is reflected in this book. So heed my warning, all who enter here. There are a few F-bombs scattered within these pages. Don't say I didn't warn you! If you require clarification on any Australian terms, please reach out. I'd love to hear from you!

The Magic and Motherhood series incorporates names of real locations in Australia that are used for authenticity but fictionalised. Please ensure you do your own research if you decide to visit these landmarks. For example (and I feel this should be self-explanatory), there is no magica sanctuary beside Australia Zoo!

If you want to keep up to date with the latest news from me, make sure you sign up to my monthly newsletter.

https://altippett.com/latest-updates/subscribe/

Thanks for taking a trip down under with me!
A. L. Tippett

Chapter One

I was going to die.

My lungs were burning, my legs were on fire, and I didn't know how much longer I could keep running. I was pretty sure I was about to paint the ground a charming shade of pink. Whoever thought it was a good idea to eat strawberries and cream on pancakes before this ordeal needed to get their head looked at. I'd be having a stern chat with Nic about her breakfast choices – if I made it out of this cave alive.

Another magica reared up out of the boulders to my right. It was a fire wyrm. If I hadn't been doing my best to avoid being brutally mauled, I would have paused to admire its iridescent crimson scales as it slithered towards me. It might have been only a few metres long, but that didn't stop my heart pounding even more loudly when its chest glowed orange as it prepared to breathe fire. Biting back a squeal, I dropped into a forward roll to avoid the flames it was spewing towards me.

Speaking of spew…

Nope, there was no time to be sick. I'd throw up once I'd finished not dying.

Regaining my feet after my roll – albeit a little clumsily – I reefed open the zipper on the bum bag attached to my armour and snatched a bead from inside it. I only had four types for this exercise, so I breathed a sigh of relief when I managed to locate the smooth blue one on my first try.

The wyrm bared its fangs and approached at speed. For a creature that had no legs, it was incredibly fast. I crushed the bead in my fist and threw up a magical shield of water just in time to protect me from a second jet of flame. The fire wyrm screeched its frustration but continued snaking forward, intent on eating me.

Ignoring my instincts that were screaming at me to run in the opposite direction, I turned and barrelled towards the magica. The legless, wingless sub-species of dragon slowed its chase and an uncharacteristic expression of confusion clouded its eyes. Even the wyrm couldn't believe what it was seeing. What an incredibly dumb move for its quarry to make – or so it must have been thinking. But I had a plan.

I just hoped it would work. Otherwise, I really might get fried.

I gritted my teeth with grim determination and plunged my hand back into the bum bag. The wyrm looked like it couldn't believe its luck when I ran straight at its gaping maw. As I leapt towards its face, it opened wide and waited for dinner to deliver itself.

Instead of handing myself over on a silver platter, I skidded to a halt in front of its snout and pulled out another bead. This one was metallic white. I smashed it between my hands and squeezed my eyes tightly shut, but even so the brilliant flash of white light it blasted out hurt my eyes.

There was a thud in front of me. I opened my eyes and blinked furiously, desperately trying to restore my vision. Fuzzy shapes started to appear. After a few more blinks I could finally see properly. The wyrm was crumpled in front of me; when I looked more closely, I noticed that its eyes had turned opaque.

All the adrenalin left my body and my legs turned to jelly. If I'd remembered my training right, it wasn't dead but merely paralysed. I allowed my legs to give way and slumped down in front of the magica, the coolness of the rock beneath me a welcome relief. Holding out my shaking hand in front of its snout, I felt its deep and steady breaths.

The fire wyrm was the third magica I'd battled that morning, and the most challenging. I was spent. Glaring at the camera in the corner of the training room that had been spelled to look like a cave, I shouted, "That's quite enough for one morning, you f— frilled-neck lizards! Let me out of here!"

There was a shimmering in the cave wall to my right and a wooden door appeared magically out of thin air. Hoisting myself off the ground with a groan, I stumbled over to it. As I glanced behind me, I tallied my battles and smiled. I'd distracted the mimic-bird with a mirror, calmed the ice-hound with the scent of lavender, and paralysed the fire wyrm with a flash bead. A year ago, that wasn't a sentence I'd thought I would ever say.

A hand clapped me on the shoulder and pulled me through the doorway. Altan's face split into a wide grin. "You did good. You should be proud. I know I am."

If my face hadn't already been red from the exertion I would have blushed at his praise.

"Barry was watching the video from his office. I know he'll have liked your work too. He wants to have a chat with you." He beckoned me to follow him.

As we walked through the halls of head office away from the battle chamber, Altan briefed me on what to expect. "Just a heads up, Barry will try to derail you with puns. Sometimes it feels like he's the office father figure and he absolutely embraces that role, Dad jokes included. Feel free to ignore them, but he'll like you even more if you have a pun for him in return. Some people say that working as an assessor over the decades has exposed him to a few too many magical attacks and addled his brain, but my theory is that he uses humour as a sort of armour. When people underestimate him, he always comes out on top."

I was panting so much after my workout with the magicas and from matching the sphinx's long stride that there wasn't much point in trying to respond. I was more than happy to let him control the conversation while I focussed on breathing. It also gave me time for the pancake-related churning in my stomach to settle down.

"Before we visit Barry, we'll do a quick detour to the lunchroom. I'm going to introduce you to the others now that you're finally at work on a weekday. Once that's done and we've seen Barry, we'll stop by Caroline to get your armour recharged."

"Recharged?"

"Yes. It works in the same way as wards on your home or car. Did you think the magic that allows it to switch between flexible and heavy duty lasts forever?"

"Erm... I hadn't really thought about it."

Altan snorted. "Righty-oh, then. Just like your security wards around your house, your armour needs to be recharged frequently otherwise the magic will fade over time. It'll vanish even faster if you're taking damage all the time, so if you've had a few hits from magicas you'll need to get it recharged sooner rather than later. Does that make sense?"

"I think so. If I'm getting beaten up by you or a magica multiple times a week, I need to visit Caroline sooner. If I'm just writing reports and interviewing people, I can wait a bit."

"That's it."

"Do you know exactly how many hits I can take?"

"No, not really. Could be three, could be ten. Depends on how big they are."

"Awesome," I said sarcastically. "That sounds super specific and easy to manage."

He grinned. "That's part of the fun."

"You and I have very different ideas of fun."

He chuckled but didn't respond as he led me up another flight of stairs. Where was an elevator when you needed one? I glared at his back suspiciously. He'd better not be avoiding elevators in an effort to improve my fitness.

We wound through the many halls of MagicAssess until we arrived in a large hall. Two long trestle tables pretty much filled the space, and there was a serving counter at one end with a large fridge filled with brightly coloured drinks beside it. I checked my watch: it was almost lunchtime. I'd been in the training session far longer than I realised.

Three figures were sitting at one of the tables and they all turned their heads towards us as we entered. The green-haired pixie, Caroline, perked up when she saw me and gave an exuberant wave. The woman and man sitting opposite her appeared to be human at first glance, but I didn't want to assume anything.

My eyes were drawn to the woman as she stood. If there was ever a person who fit the description of 'battle-hardened', it was she. Leathery face, crow's feet, callouses, muscles upon muscles; she wore them all like they were part of her uniform. Her hair had been shaved into a buzz cut and she was dressed in full armour. Although she was older than me by maybe a decade, she looked like she had the ability to kill me before I even thought about taking another step.

When I'd taken on the job of insurance assessor, I had half-expected the soft middles and pale skin that were the usual fair for deskbound workers. I'd certainly never imagined warrior-princess vibes from my new colleagues.

My steps faltered as I approached. She was one intimidating lady. I didn't even know if I was brave enough to call her a lady.

She probably preferred to go by 'ripper' or 'warrior', or something equally frightening.

Striding towards me, she thrust out her hand and I flinched before shaking it. Her grip nearly crushed my fingers. I resisted the urge to flex my fingers and check they weren't all broken after she released me. "So," she drawled, "this is the new recruit?" She had a distinct Kiwi accent; she must have been from New Zealand originally.

"Yup!" Caroline was endlessly enthusiastic and didn't seem to notice the terror in my eyes. She danced over to me, stretched up onto her tiptoes and pecked me on the cheek. "Good to see you, lovely," she chirped. "Everyone, this is Trix. Trix, this is everyone." She gave a tinkling laugh, then took pity on me and pointed at the woman. "This is Rosalyn, one of the senior assessors at MagicAssess."

The woman wrinkled her nose and corrected the pixie. "Just call me Ros."

"T...Tr...Trix," I stammered. My cheeks warmed and I cleared my throat before trying again. "My name is Beatrix, but everyone calls me Trix." I glanced between her and the pixie. "But Caroline already told you that." I was suddenly conscious that I probably stank from sweating through my ordeal in the battle chamber. So much for good first impressions.

Caroline snorted. "Yeah, I did, but I failed to mention that Ros is the boss's daughter." She gave a wicked cackle at the death stare Ros gave her.

I stared at my friend in horror. *I* would never feel safe laughing in that woman's face. Ros crossed her arms and shook her head in disgust. "You know I hate it when you introduce me like that. Yes, Barry is my father, but just because I'm the boss's daughter doesn't mean I get any special treatment. You can bet your ass that I'll be working as hard as the next person." She spoke somewhat defensively, and I wondered what had happened in the past to make her so prickly about her relationship to Barry.

Caroline grinned at her testiness.

Altan smirked but, unlike Caroline, I was certain he could sense my apprehension. He said, "Trix has just impressed your dad in the battle chamber. Obviously, that's all thanks to me and my impressive training skills." He crossed his arms smugly.

Ros looked me up and down and raised an eyebrow. I gulped: she was terrifying.

I'd almost forgotten about the dark-haired guy who'd been standing off to the side but now he approached and held out his hand. He appeared to be in his thirties, and there was something about his face that instantly made me think of a slug. His grip was weak, especially compared to Ros's, and I struggled not to judge him immediately.

"I'm Dave," he said with an air of authority. "I've just come back from finalising a job." He put his hands on his hips and puffed out his chest.

I noticed that his hair was carefully styled; I wouldn't have thought that people who were regularly battling magicas would use that much product, but what did I know?

"Got it all tied up in less than twelve hours. I think that might be a new record," he gloated.

Ros snorted. "You might have finalised your paperwork, boy, but did you actually do it right this time?" she countered.

I saw his hackles rise at her condescending tone and he shot her a sullen expression. His attitude was worse than a teen – and I should know. My teenage daughter was a saint compared to him.

"That wasn't my fault," he seethed. "If that woman had just accepted responsibility..."

"Ha!" Ros barked a laugh. "Like you can lecture about accepting responsibility!" She turned her back on Dave and returned her attention to me. "Altan gave me the lowdown about what happened in Bowen. Your first claim was pretty full on. How are you holding up?"

Her accent was strong, but her warm tone surprised me. Maybe she was a softie at heart, like a Doberman. They might look as if they could eat you alive, but they were really just big teddy bears.

"I was exhausted when we got back," I said. "After we flew home, Altan made me use a healing bead and I slept for more than twelve hours. I was still lethargic the next day, so I spent my first day at home filling out the report and napping. But it was worth it to get to the bottom of it."

I paused, unsure how much I should open up to the boss's daughter but then dismissed the thought; that was probably why she didn't like to tell people about their relationship. "The claim itself was... Well, it was pretty overwhelming, but I learnt a lot." I shrugged nonchalantly, doing my best to fit in with the cool kids. "Plus, I got to eat mango sorbet, so it was a win-win."

Ros snorted. "Nice. Mango sorbet always makes life better."

Dave's phone rang, interrupting the conversation. He excused himself to answer it.

Altan squeezed my shoulder. "Sorry, ladies, but we must keep going. We're off to have a chat to Barry, but since you're here, Caroline, can you arrange to recharge Trix's armour sometime this week?"

The pixie gave a jaunty salute. "Certainly can, Altan."

"Perfect. Thank you. Trix, let's go."

I gave an awkward wave to my new colleagues, then breathed a sigh of relief as we left the lunchroom. That could have gone much worse. My first official day at head office wasn't turning out so badly after all.

Chapter Two

THE SOFT GLOW OF a fish tank was the first thing I noticed when we arrived outside Barry's office. It was set into the hallway wall beside an open door that offered a glimpse inside the room. The blue LED light and soft current pushing the live coral around told me it was a saltwater tank.

I admired the healthy-looking clownfish and blue tangs. It wasn't many years ago that my daughter would have been gleefully telling everyone about how she'd seen Dory and Nemo. Of course she was too old for that now.

I sighed. How quickly the years disappeared. It felt like only yesterday that Millie had been relying on me to survive, and now she was a young woman getting ready to forge her own path.

I shook my head to stop my reminiscing and walked through the open door with Altan following behind me. I was immediately impressed by the wall-to-wall bookshelves. Some of the titles looked to be insurance-related textbooks, but quite a few of them were about spell craft and magica breeds. My mouth dropped open. What I wouldn't give to chill out in here for a few days and do nothing but read.

A large glass window took up the fourth wall behind the massive mahogany desk. The man sitting at the computer monitor stood. He looked to be in his sixties, with light stubble and silver flecks through his dark hair. As the boss, I'd half-expected him to wear a suit but he was dressed in the same style of armour as I was.

As he closed in on us, his grey eyes exuded warmth. He stuck out his hand. "Nice to finally meet you, Trix. Altan's told me all about you. I'm Barry Keeling, head assessor, trainer and safety officer at MagicAssess."

My eyebrows shot up. "That's a lot of hats."

He chuckled. "I've always liked hats. My personal favourite is a fedora."

I frowned. "Wait, what?" Glancing at Altan, I stage whispered, "Why are we talking about hats?"

Altan snickered then murmured, "Remember what I said."

A-ha: the dad jokes had already begun. But if this was a test to see how I tolerated them, I couldn't let him derail me. I narrowed my eyes a little before waving my hand towards his armour. "I'm not here to talk about hats. But speaking of things we put on our bodies, I see that you are wearing armour. Are you heading out to a job?"

His eyes twinkled at my redirection before he shook his head. "Always be prepared. It's the assessor's motto."

"Ah, yes. Altan has drilled that one into me."

Barry smiled. "I don't doubt it. As I'm sure Altan has also explained to you, the industry is in crisis and we're trying hard to employ more assessors to ease the load on the existing ones."

He cast a hand back towards his computer screen. The battle chamber where I'd been fighting magicas was still on display. "On that note, I've got to say not bad, kid." He scrubbed a hand over his silver stubble. "Not bad at all."

His tone was complimentary and, combined with his Kiwi accent, made my insides feel all warm and fuzzy. Altan was right: Barry *was* like a father figure.

"You've been training with Altan for a couple of months now, yeah?" he asked.

"Five weeks," I corrected.

"You're a quick study. Sure, there's a lot of work to be done but it's a solid foundation. Keep at it. Let me know if you need additional support and I'll see what we can do. We're a family here, and we look out for each other."

Altan piped up. "I've found her natural ability to assess danger and take instinctive action remarkable for someone with no prior training. Her skillset needs to be expanded and, as we discussed before she came onboard, her relevant job experience is non-existent but she did brilliantly with the missing mango claim. She's an asset to the team."

I gave a bashful smile at his compliment and butterflies erupted in my stomach. I did my best to tamp them down; I should not be reacting this strongly to his compliments.

Barry nodded slowly. "I can see that. I have high hopes for you, kid."

"Thank you, sir."

"We don't stand on ceremony here. Barry is fine." He strode back to his desk and picked up his mobile phone. "Don't go anywhere, I have a job for you both. But first..." He tapped the screen and held the phone to his ear. "Dave, get up here now," he barked.

I watched his demeanour change as he went from warm father figure to cold soldier in a matter of seconds. I shivered. Note to self: don't get on the wrong side of this man.

Barry hung up and put down his phone before picking up a thin manila folder and my work tablet from the desk. Altan and I shared a quizzical look. Why was Dave being summoned when we were getting a job? Had I done something wrong? Was he wanting someone else to train me?

My stomach dropped. What if he ordered me to pair with Dave for the next job? The thought of not working with Altan was terrible, especially while I was still finding my feet.

Barry passed the folder to Altan and the tablet to me. "Before we talk about this claim, I want to discuss your ongoing training, Trix."

He perched on the edge of his desk, but he didn't invite us to take a seat, so I assumed we wouldn't be there much longer. "Based on the video footage of your time in the battle chamber, I'd say your fitness is on track. It could certainly be improved, but considering Altan said you've been stuck behind a desk or at home with your kid for more than a decade, I'd say you're doing pretty well. But don't slack off. I need you to be able to outrun a harpy before the next round in there, okay?"

I gulped but nodded anyway. Frick-a-fracking frog's legs. I really didn't want to face a harpy.

"Considering how you dealt with the three different magicas in there today, your general knowledge about magical creatures appears to be solid. Keep studying, though. There's always more to learn. You never know when a random piece of information will save your ass. However, I want you to do more combat training. You need a broad knowledge of ranged and melee weapons, as well as hand-to-hand."

He looked at Altan. "Maybe have her focus on your preferred combat style to start with. With the workload we have right now, you might need to train outside office hours. I'm sorry about that, but keep track of your extra hours and we'll compensate you."

I held up my hand. "Wait a sec. Are you saying you're going to pay me to exercise?"

Barry grinned, but Altan interrupted before he could respond. "Don't get too excited, Trix. We'll start off by learning Brazilian

Jiu Jitsu for self-defence. Trust me, you'll be cursing Barry and his overtime money for the first few weeks when you're in constant pain from the new muscles you'll be using."

My head swivelled between the two men as I tried to figure out if they were joking.

Before I could work it out, there was a loud knock at the door and Dave walked in. The temperature in the room dropped and the smile on Barry's face disappeared. He crossed his arms and waited silently for Dave to stop beside Altan. Then he said abruptly, "We've got a problem, Dave. I want to talk about the claim for the fire damage at the magica sanctuary that operates beside Australia Zoo in Beerwah. Based on what I could understand of your notes, it appears you have ruled it as natural causes?"

Dave shrugged dispassionately. "Yeah. It was a bushfire that broke the wards and caused some damage."

The icy glare that Barry directed at Dave had me shaking in my boots. "A bushfire," he repeated slowly. "A bushfire that broke the wards that were placed there specifically to avoid fire damage."

He took a deep breath. "Having reviewed your report, I can see no reason why you dismissed it as natural. There is still a small chance that it was just a bushfire, but I see a lot more that suggests it was arson, possibly magical based. You didn't even interview the employees."

The sullen pout on Dave's lips made him even more unattractive. "It's not my fault," he whined. "The fire brigade ruled it as natural causes and the police aren't suspicious, so what's the problem?"

Barry's eyes narrowed and I was glad his disappointment wasn't being turned on me. "The human beings, who have limited magical training, have ruled it as natural so that means you don't need to do your job?" Sarcasm dripped from every word.

Dave attempted to mimic Barry's posture by crossing his arms and puffing himself up. "Just tell the insurer to pay the claim. What does it matter?"

"Our job is to provide a comprehensive report on all claims that come through our door. Excellence in this job isn't optional, it is expected. You know that."

"Piss off!"

I flinched at the venom in Dave's voice. How he dared to speak like that to the boss was beyond me.

Barry frowned and took a step forward. "Careful, Dave," he growled.

"Nah, this is fucked," Dave retaliated. "I've busted my ass for you for years. MagicAssess is losing people every year, meaning we all have to work overtime to keep up with the claims. We need more staff and all you've done is import this Pommie prick." He glared at Altan. "And now you've taken on an unqualified and incompetent sheila! Fuck this. I'm taking my annual leave. Sort your shit out or I won't come back."

He stormed out of the office, slamming the door behind him. A heavy silence hung in the air for a few long seconds. I realised my mouth was catching flies, so I hurriedly clipped it shut.

Altan glared at the door and muttered, "He is a major problem."

Sighing, Barry rubbed a hand over his face. "He might be, but we shouldn't be too tough on him. He took Jessica's death harder than anyone else here." He glanced at me. "She was the latest assessor to lose her life. And he does have a point. We *do* need more staff."

He suddenly sounded weary. "It's a vicious circle. I need to employ more people but those people have to be properly trained and I don't have the spare staff to focus on training new recruits. If we put on too many at once and don't provide adequate training, the mortality rate among assessors will rise. We're screwed if we do and screwed if we don't."

He flopped down in his black-leather office chair. "This is why I'm hoping this experiment with you two will work: intensive on-the-job training so we don't wind up with a backlog of claims while you get to learn the ropes under supervision." He raised his eyebrows at me. "I really need to make this work so we can bring in new people. Please don't die, Trix."

I snorted. "I'm not planning on it," I said.

At the same time, Altan muttered, "I won't let her."

Clearing his throat, Barry waved at the file. "Back to the claim."

I pressed the home button on my tablet while Altan opened the folder and examined the paper version. The file was already open on my screen, so I flicked through the few photos that Dave had snapped while Altan looked at the printouts.

"I've reassigned the file to your account, Trix," Barry said, "but I wanted to give a quick verbal handover about the claim. Last week, a fire broke out at the Magica Sanctuary of Queensland, damaging a boundary fence and some of the enclosures. No deaths or injuries of humans or creatures were reported, and nothing was stolen. As you heard, the fire service, the police, and Dave have all ruled the fire as having natural causes.

"The claim that's been lodged is only for property damage. We need to ensure it wasn't started deliberately by the owners because the insurer won't cover arson. We also need to review their policy to make sure there are no limits or exclusions to their cover. Lastly, we have to make sure that the figure they're claiming is fair and reasonable for the damage sustained. The report that Dave has provided is very basic. I'll admit he's not my best employee, but this is scant even by his standards."

He shrugged. "Grief does funny things to people." When Altan snorted, Barry gently reprimanded him. "Try not to judge him too harshly. Give him some time to get his head back on straight."

"You're too nice, Barry," said Altan.

"I'll remember that next time you ask for annual leave," our boss said with a grin. "There's a small chance that Dave is right and it's not arson, but my gut is saying it was. However, was it a random attack that the insurer will cover, or was it started by the owner or an employee? That's what I need you to figure out."

Feeling uncertain about the job, I blew out a steadying breath. I caught Barry's eye and offered a tentative smile. His features softened.

"Try not to stress too much," he told me. "You've got Altan to guide you, and I'm here if you need anything else. So long as there are no dragons or drop bears hanging about, I'm sure you'll be fine." He flashed a smile. "Good luck! And remember what I told you."

I frowned. "Which part?"

"Don't die."

CHAPTER THREE

"There's no time like the present," Altan announced as soon as we left Barry's office. "Let's head off now and take care of the initial interviews."

It didn't take us long to navigate our way out of the city of Brisbane onto the M1, which we followed north. It would take close to an hour of driving on the highway to reach our destination. I wondered if we could head straight back home to Maroochydore from there since Altan had driven me to work that morning.

My personal phone pinged with a text message.

Mum – Valerie Greenstone

I'll see you and Millie later tonight.

Anger immediately curdled in my gut as I stared at the text from my mother. I hadn't heard from her since she'd announced she was coming to visit after Altan and I had closed the claim for the Big Mango. I'd texted and called her to find out when precisely

I could expect her and had no response. Now she was just breezing in with no notice and no thought of anyone else's needs.

I frowned as I reread the message. Was I supposed to pick her up from the airport? Was she meeting us at our house? "I've got to make a phone call," I said to Altan.

My call to my mother went straight to voicemail and I harrumphed as I waited for her recorded message to end. Finally I was able to ask her to call me back so I knew what the plan was, then I texted her and even followed through with an email for good measure. I stared at the screen for a minute but gave up when there was no reply.

I threw my phone into my handbag a little more viciously than it deserved. Altan glanced at me before returning his focus to the road. "Do you want to talk about it?"

"Nope," I said curtly and stared sullenly out the window.

The silence stretched between us for a few minutes. Finally, I pushed my worries about my mother out of my head. It wasn't Altan's fault that she was a flaky piece of poop, and I shouldn't take my frustrations out on him. Clearing my throat, I said, "So, let's discuss the claim. Where is this sanctuary? Did Barry say something about it being connected with Australia Zoo?"

"Sort of. The Magica Sanctuary of Queensland, or MSQ, is its own entity but is situated beside Australia Zoo in Beerwah. The zoo handles the mundane animals while the sanctuary helps injured or ill magicas on their road to recovery and eventually to return to the wild."

"That's awesome! I hadn't heard about the sanctuary, but I love Australia Zoo!" I gushed. "I haven't been there for years but it used to be awesome. That's Irwin's legacy. Everybody loved Steve."

I put on a stronger than usual Aussie accent and exclaimed, "Crikey, mate, she's a beauty!" Colour tinged my cheeks as I suddenly became self-conscious at my poor impersonation skills. If my daughter could hear me, she'd absolutely call me out as being 'cringe'.

Altan didn't say anything about my very average acting. "I heard good things about him, but we never met and I've never been to Australia Zoo before. I'm not sure that I agree with zoos, but the sanctuary is a different kettle of fish."

He pursed his lips. "At the end of the day, it's not our job to pass judgement. We're there to find the truth about what happened. We may experience some pushback since Dave's already been, but take my lead and hold fast to your resolve. We need our questions answered."

After around forty-five minutes, we turned off the highway onto Steve Irwin Way, past the sign for Beerburrum and through Beerwah until we saw the sign for Australia Zoo.

"Do they really like drinking beer around here?" Altan asked suddenly.

I gave a bark of laughter before I could stop myself. "No more than most other Queenslanders. No, a lot of the names are derived from the indigenous people's languages. I don't know what it means because I never learnt any, I'm afraid." I shrugged apologetically. "But Millie has been taught some of the language at school. There's a much bigger push to educate kids about Australia's Aboriginal culture compared to when I was in school. I should get Millie to teach me," I mused.

"That makes sense," Altan replied. "Although with some of the interesting choices that Australians make, it wouldn't have surprised me if it *was* named just because of the beer."

"Hey, we're not all alcoholics!" I said in mock offence.

He snorted then ignored me as he slowed down. Instead of parking in the zoo's carpark, he drove to the northern end where a gravel road with a metal gate blocked us. Before he had a chance to unbuckle himself, I leapt out of the car and unfastened the gate's chain. Swinging the gate open, I waited for him to pull through before I shut it again and hopped back in.

"Thanks," he said then paused as if he wanted to say more.

Studying him, I asked, "What?"

"It's nice to work with someone who takes the initiative about the basic things."

My brows pulled together. "It wasn't even that helpful."

"It was," he replied softly, his eyes staying on the gravel drive.

I chuckled. "You're welcome, I guess. You must have worked with some very self-absorbed people."

"You have no idea."

Before I could ask for more details, we parked in front of a faded sign that announced we had arrived at the Magica Sanctuary of Queensland. A smaller white sign with black writing pointed us left to the office.

Feeling out of my depth, I took a deep breath and willed the nerves in my stomach to settle. This wasn't my first rodeo – though admittedly it was only my second. But I could do this, and I had Altan to pick me up when I fell. In my mind there was no 'if'; I definitely needed more on-the-job experience before anyone let me loose on my own.

Unbuckling my seat belt, I collected my bag containing the work tablet, together with Altan's handy-dandy notepad, and joined him at the back of the car. He opened the boot, buckled on a sword, and handed me the spatha I had trained with last month. I attached the short sword and its leather scabbard onto my belt. Looking around, I noted there were only three vehicles in the carpark: an aged red hatchback, a cream van with a vet's logo on it, and a white ute.

Readjusting the bag on my shoulder, we walked away from the carpark and towards the sign for the office. Palm trees stood like sentinels beside the big sign, while the gum trees hugging the carpark provided ample shade. The tan leaves fluttered around our feet in the slight breeze.

Altan waved me ahead of him and I followed a dirt path edged with spider lilies. I paused for a beat. Spider lilies? I guessed it was another of those random facts about plants that I didn't remember learning. I'd have to ask Altan if he'd heard anything back from his connection about my weird abilities.

I was so focussed on the plants that, for a moment, I didn't realise I was standing in front of the office. I sighed as I took it in.

"What's wrong?" asked Altan.

I screwed up my face as if I'd eaten a lemon. "It's a donga."

"I beg your pardon. A what?"

"The most bogan word I've ever had the displeasure of having to use." I waved a hand at the iron-clad box in front of me. "It's a donga." I placed emphasis on the 'ng' sound, pushing the nasal tone harder than needed.

"A transportable building," I explained. "Technically, there's nothing wrong with them. They're functional and they're cheaper than building a permanent structure, I just have a problem with the word. The English language is amazing in that it can weave such magic, yet donga is the word they came up with for this." I gave the cream-coloured structure that sat on stumps a melancholy look.

The sphinx stared at me for a long moment until his cat-like ears flicked. "Sometimes you're a little odd. Did you know that?"

"Only a little?"

He chuckled, and I melted at the sound. Pushing open the office door, he held it open for me. Focussing on the job at hand, I didn't allow myself to think about the heat radiating off his skin as I brushed past him.

As we stepped inside, I quickly analysed the room. It was the definition of tired. A white pedestal fan feebly tried to move air around the space; it looked like the air-conditioning unit wasn't working. A few small photos of Steve Irwin with different creatures, both native and magical, dotted the walls. An overflowing filing cabinet sat in the corner behind a black desk on which there was a desktop computer and a plastic filing tray. I could see a lot of overdue bills with angry red letters stamped across the top nestling in the container.

At the back of the room there was a fridge and a basic kitchenette with dirty dishes stacked beside the sink. A couple of lounge chairs were on my left beside a lonely plant that looked like it needed a good water and some fertiliser.

A man popped his head up from behind the computer monitor. His skin was oddly pale and he had dark circles under his eyes. He stood up with a groan and came out from behind his desk to greet us.

"Good morning, guys. I'm Todd. I received a call earlier from MagicAssess, so I guess I can safely assume you're the new team?"

Altan nodded and introduced us before adding smoothly, "We apologise for taking up your valuable time after one of our colleagues has already attended the site. There were a few discrepancies in his report that we'd like to review."

"Of course," Todd replied amiably. "Not that I know what's involved in your job, but I did think he was in and out surprisingly fast. I told him I had a hunch the fire wasn't started by natural causes but he didn't seem to want to hear it." He grinned sheepishly. "Sorry, I know he's your colleague. I'm sure he's good at his job."

He raked his hands through his strawberry-blond hair making it stick up in uneven, spiky tufts. I bit back a laugh. "Although, if he was good at his job," he went on, "you wouldn't be here. He was a bit of a—" He cut himself off and chuckled nervously. "You know what, I'm going to stop talking. How can I help?"

I couldn't stop myself from snorting. Altan raised an eyebrow at me and I quickly turned it into a cough. Returning his attention to Todd, the sphinx said, "We've reviewed the file but can you tell us what happened in your own words? And what was your hunch?"

"Last week Clyde woke me up with a call at six o'clock in the morning to say there was a bushfire at the boundary fence between the kapamu and griffin enclosures." I opened my mouth to interrupt, but Todd pre-empted my question. "Clyde is our resident handyman. He's a gnome, and usually drunk no matter the time of day, but he fixes problems quickly. I turn a blind eye to the drinking, and he gets shit done – fixing fences, doing electrical work, setting up security cameras, mowing the lawn – you name it, he probably does it." Todd glanced at the air con. "I need to get him back in the office though. I won't survive summer without that."

Shaking his head, he returned to his story. "I raced down here but the fire department already had it under control. There was some damage to the perimeter fence as well as one of the habitats, and a couple of the magicas had to be vetted for smoke inhalation. The claim we submitted was for the fire damage to the sanctuary, the broken ward replacement, and I also asked our insurer if we could claim the vet bill." He shrugged. "The police took our statements. There's not much else to tell."

I was busy making notes on the tablet as he spoke. Altan probed, "You mentioned you had a hunch about the incident?"

Todd mussed his hair again, the stress on his face evident. "The police, the firies—" at Altan's frown, Todd clarified, "—the firefighters, and the other assessor seemed to think it was just a random bushfire. They claimed there was no evidence of an accelerant." He hesitated, his eyes darting between us.

"And you don't think it was natural," I prompted.

"No disrespect to the professionals, but my gut says no. The path of the fire is too straight to be natural. The firies said that can happen when the wind blows just right, but it seems weird to me.

But maybe I'm wrong." He gave a humourless chuckle. "Maybe the stress has finally broken my brain."

Altan turned to me. "All right, Trix, you take lead. What do you want to do?"

Panic at suddenly being put on the spot gnawed at my insides, but I squashed it deep down. Fake it 'til you make it, and all that. I said firmly, "First, can we inspect the site of the fire and the associated damage?" Todd nodded. "And I'll need to take some more photos for the report. Do I have your permission to do that?"

"Absolutely."

I glanced down at my tablet. "Can you send through the invoices or quotes that you have for the repairs?"

"Of course. I received a quote this morning from the fencing contractor, but I'm still waiting on a quote to replace the broken wards. I've also contacted the druid ambassador to request they repair some of the shaping work. I'm not sure how much that will cost, but I'll send through the quotes as I receive them."

What the heck was shaping work? I'd have to ask Altan later.

I continued as if I knew what he was talking about. "Excellent. Another thing. Australia Zoo is next door. Do you have any connection or shared resources?"

"No, we're a completely separate entity. To my knowledge, we don't share any employees, suppliers or security systems. Australia Zoo is for non-magical animals, whilst our sanctuary helps rehabilitate injured or sick wild magicas and return them to their natural habitat."

"Thanks for clarifying that. I'll need a list of the sanctuary's employees and their contact details, plus anyone who might have had access to the site or who you think might hold a grudge against you or the sanctuary."

Altan looked quite impressed and I gave myself an imaginary pat on the back. See, I could do this. I just needed to trust myself.

Todd looked relieved to hear that someone was finally taking him seriously. "Of course." He nodded enthusiastically. "This way." He walked past us, opened the door and beckoned us forward.

"What did the police do when they were here? Did they interview everyone?" Altan asked.

Todd screwed up his face. "Not that I know of." He paused and studied us for a long moment. "My husband..." he began slowly before clearing his throat. "My husband, James, is a satyr, and he was with me when I was making my report. I'm not sure that the authorities are as accepting of cross-species relationships as they claim to be."

Altan sighed unhappily. "So what you're saying is you think they treated you like garbage because they believe you're married to an animal just because James has hooves."

Todd barked a harsh laugh. "I wasn't going to put it quite so bluntly, but yeah, pretty much."

"I'm sorry to hear that you were treated like that," I said.

He shrugged and mumbled, "We're used to it."

"So are we," Altan muttered.

Shooting him a look, Todd's head swivelled between the sphinx and me before a look of understanding dawned on his face. I blushed and quickly corrected his assumption. "What my colleague means is that we've frequently seen this kind of disregard for magicas' rights from the authorities in other claims. We'll do everything we can to help."

"LET ME SHOW YOU around," Todd said.

We left the donga and he led us down a gravel path that was wide enough for a vehicle. Large native trees cast their shadows over us, and different species of ferns and shrubs hugged the path's border, making it feel like we were in a rainforest. Birds trilled in the trees and the air smelt fresh as if a rainstorm had just passed through. There was some fencing running through the foliage, and Todd explained that each enclosure housed a different species of magica.

He gestured to our left. "That paddock has three kapamus. They look like emus but they're much shorter. You probably can't see them because they blend in well with their habitat, but don't relax. They're as lethal as a crocodile crossed with a cassowary. One kapamu is scheduled to be released back into the wild next week, one is currently undergoing treatment for a recurring infection, and the third will remain in captivity until its death because it was plucked while it was still alive."

He shook his head in disgust. "It's sick what humans will do in the name of the greater good. Who plucks a bird while it's alive and leaves it to die a slow death from exposure? They poach these magicas and harvest the parts that are most useful to them because they claim it will help humankind. But at what cost?"

As we passed the kapamus' enclosure, it was obvious where the fire had broken the wards. A two-metre section of the boundary fence had burned away and a temporary fence of plastic orange webbing erected in the gap.

Todd pointed past the fencing at the blackened earth. His earlier comment appeared to be right: it looked like the fire had travelled in a straight line up to the fence before hitting the boundary. There was a bluish residue in the shape of a starburst on the ground where the fire protection ward had broken.

I raised the tablet and took some photos. Pulling out a bead, Altan threw it into the centre of the starburst. It immediately turned a vibrant pink. He looked disappointed as he turned to Todd. "On behalf of MagicAssess, I'd like to apologise for our colleague's earlier work. The wards have been broken magically, so I can definitely state that this damage was not caused by a simple bushfire. Dave should never have closed the file. We understand that the humans who work with the fire brigade and police don't have the resources or magical knowledge to check for these things, so we'll advise them that they need to reopen the case."

He glanced at me before returning his gaze to Todd. "They don't always take kindly to being told they're wrong but rest assured; if they offer resistance, Trix and I will assist in finding the perpetrator and ensure they didn't do anything else after they gained access."

"I appreciate that," Todd replied. "I'm just glad someone is taking it seriously. To be honest, I feel like I've been banging my head against a brick wall. No one seemed to believe that it was anything other than an accidental bushfire."

"That must have been frustrating," I said. "Is there anyone you suspect that might have started the fire on purpose?"

Todd frowned and stroked his chin. "I can't come up with anyone off the top of my head, but I'll have another think about it. I'll help in any way I can, so just let me know what you need and I'll get it for you."

"For now, a tour of the sanctuary and interviews with employees or any persons of interest would be a great start," Altan told him.

"And we'll need the name of the officer in charge of the investigation and the police report number," I added.

"I'll get those for you when we're back in the office. In the meantime, let me show you the rest of the grounds." Once we were back on the main path, Todd nodded to the right. "That's our winged magica enclosure. We only have one griffin at the moment. He's got an infection in his tail from a partial amputation."

A shiver ran down my spine at his words. As I stared into the undergrowth, yellow eyes stared back at me and I jerked to a stop. When an unearthly scream shattered the day's stillness, fear immediately pierced my heart at the familiar cry and set my teeth on edge.

My head whipped back and forth as I tried to locate the danger. Something was crashing through the bush in the enclosure beside me, getting closer and closer. I automatically unsheathed my spatha and unzipped my bum bag, telling myself I was ready for whatever was coming.

Todd shot me an amused expression. "It's okay. No magical creature can escape from these enclosures. The druids came when the sanctuary was being built, shaped a living barrier and wove their magic into it. Their magic makes the fence stronger than anything man-made and it'll stop any creature getting out."

Still shrieking, the griffin crashed closer. I reluctantly lowered my short sword.

"You're perfectly safe," Todd went on. "Although I don't know why he's in a huff. I've barely heard him squawk since he arrived."

"Who is 'he'?" I asked, pleased that I'd managed to keep the tremble out of my voice.

"We took custody of the griffin about a month ago. The wound that he was brought in for has healed nicely, but he's had ongoing problems with infections that we've had to treat. He's almost ready to return to the wild now, though."

I found a gap in the branches that made up the perimeter fence and peered through. A giant, brown, feathery body loomed into my vision and hurled itself at the boundary fence.

"Blimey," I exclaimed and leapt backwards, my sword automatically swinging into a defensive position. I frowned when the yellow eyes peered through the thick foliage at me. I was certain they'd been green at the netball courts but, even so, I knew it was him. I would never forget the colour of his feathers or the lethal point of his beak, nor the image of Altan slicing his tail to distract him from attacking my daughter.

Altan was standing close to me, ready to protect all of us regardless of Todd's assurances. He saw me freeze. "What is it?" he hissed.

My heart pounded and my breathing accelerated. I didn't know how I knew, but I replied with certainty, "It's him."

His brows pulling together, Altan scanned the bush as he sought our would-be attacker. "Who?" he whispered.

"The griffin that attacked us at the netball courts."

"Are you kidding me?" he exclaimed.

Looking between us and the griffin, Todd asked, "This fellow attacked you on the outside?"

Altan's lips thinned. "Unfortunately, I must confess that I'm the one who hurt him. It was a matter of life and death for Trix and her daughter, and I did all that I could to save them and the other civilians before resorting to physical violence."

He moved into a position where the griffin could see him then placed his hand on his heart and bowed low. He stayed frozen in that position for more than twenty seconds while the magica surveyed him before grudgingly bobbing his head and turning his back on us. Then he disappeared into the bush once more.

Todd stared between us and the empty space where the griffin had been, his head whipping back and forth. "Well...that's...he... I..." he sputtered before clearing his throat. "That's not something you see every day."

He gazed at us a little longer before turning on his heel. "Let me show you the stables. We keep our earth-based magicas in the paddock but allow them access to the stables at night. When they're injured, we can confine them to stall rest. We currently have two unicorns in care."

There was a large, iron-clad shed around the next corner. As we entered it, Todd showed us the fully stocked storeroom of potions beside the entrance next to the stalls.

"Anything missing?" asked Altan.

"I haven't completed a full inventory, but there's nothing obvious. That door was still locked when I arrived on the morning of the fire." Todd continued down the breezeway between the stalls towards the sound of hushed voices. The scent of lucerne hay, fresh shavings, and manure filled the air. He stopped in front of the last stall door.

Two women in dark-blue coveralls were sitting beside a pale-yellow unicorn who was lying on a bed of wood shavings. The unicorn's eyes were closed, and her barrel looked bloated. She uttered a soft groan as the older woman gently laid the magica's head on the floor. Slowly, both women stood and crept out of the stall.

We automatically moved away from the sleeping unicorn before Todd introduced us. Waving at the older woman, he said, "This is Anna, our on-call vet who specialises in magicas. This is her sister, Becky, who also works as her assistant." He nodded towards the unicorn's stall. "Unfortunately, one of our rescues slipped her foal this morning and these ladies have been trying to ease her suffering. Unicorns feel grief the same way we do, and she's not handling the loss of her foal well. Anna and Becky have given her a sedative to help her get some much-needed rest."

Anna's eyebrows pinched together, and she tried unsuccessfully to flatten her frizzy blonde hair. "Not to sound rude, but who are you?"

Altan held out his hand. "I'm Altan and this is Trix. We're insurance assessors from MagicAssess, here about the claim for the fire damage."

Becky was a pale waif of a thing, especially compared to the stockiness of her sister. Her hair was a more platinum shade than Anna's and it lay obediently flat against her skull. Her arms were crossed but her tone was gentle when she asked, "Wasn't there already an assessor here?"

I wondered how many times we'd have to repeat our story without outing Dave as incompetent. "We need to take another look because the initial report wasn't as thorough as we'd have liked. Did either of you notice anything unusual while you were here on the day of the fire?"

"I didn't attend that day. I was sick," Becky replied. "But Anna didn't mention anything weird to me." She turned and craned her neck to look up at her taller sister.

"I wasn't called in until after the police and firies had already arrived," explained Anna. "There were a lot of people milling around, and the magicas were unsettled, but I was just here to do my job. I spent all morning making sure that they weren't hurt or suffering from smoke inhalation, so I didn't pay attention to what the humans were doing." She shrugged. "Sorry I can't be of more help."

I passed her a business card. "If you do think of anything, please don't hesitate to get in touch."

"Sure thing," she replied. Glancing at her phone, she asked, "Do you have any other questions? It's just that we need to get going to our next job."

"We'd like an accurate timeline of your movements and the names of anyone you did happen to notice or interact with. If you could email those to us, that would be very helpful."

Anna nodded brusquely. "Can do," she said before picking up her supply bag and heading out of the stables.

Becky gave a demure smile and trailed after her sister.

Chapter Five

Todd led us away from the resting unicorn's stall and opened a door to the feed room. Large blue wheelie bins lined the walls and he opened the lids to show us the animal feed. There were pellets, chaff, powders, along with bales of hay and a plastic pod of thick brown liquid.

I was wondering if it was some magical ointment when the smell hit me: vaguely sweet with a slightly sour, earthy undertone. I wrinkled my nose and pointed. "What is that?"

Todd chuckled. "It's molasses, a by-product of sugar production and loved by mundane creatures and magicas alike."

I coughed. While the smell was not entirely unpleasant, it *was* very strong. "Are you sure they like it?"

"It takes some getting used to when you haven't smelt it before, but I promise you the creatures love it. Makes it really easy to manage them. I just bring out a bucket of molasses and most of them will follow me anywhere."

As he showed Altan the small black camera in the corner of the room, I rested my tablet on a wheelie bin's lid and typed in some notes. My focus was interrupted by a heavy weight unexpectedly landing on my shoulders.

A screech ripped out of my throat as my brain registered the sleek coils draped around my neck. I tried to lift my arms to rid myself of the serpent that had decided to turn me into a perch but a churlish voice in my head stopped me. *"Quit your flailing, silly lady. I ain't gonna hurt you."*

At my scream, Altan spun around and bounded toward me. He reached for the snake.

"Stop," I managed to pant out. My heart had learnt the samba in the last few seconds and was dancing to its own rhythm in my chest. I closed my eyes and tried not to have a panic attack. Snakes were a common part of Australian life, and I'd heard of them occasionally dropping out of rafters or vents onto people, but that didn't mean I wanted one draped around me.

Todd grinned. "Oh, that's just Harry. He's our resident pest controller."

"I prefer Harrison," sniffed the black, brown, and white coloured snake as he wound his way up my arm and paused at my wrist, his tongue flicking.

I supposed the peculiar diamond-shaped pattern along his back would be quite beautiful, if I wasn't so focussed on not having a heart attack.

Todd moved towards me with an easy smile; he was probably trying to keep me calm. "He's a carpet python," he explained. "He won't hurt you. At least, he won't so long as he doesn't strangle you."

"Not hungry anyway," said the snake in my head. *"Ate a couple o' rats last night."* He raised his head a little to look in my eyes. *"I hear you humans talk. You all talk so much. You and the cat are new here. You came because o' the fire?"* he asked. I gave a subtle nod. His

forked tongue flicked again, tickling my wrist. *"Honey,"* he added then reared up aggressively as Altan and Todd stepped closer to me.

I stared at Altan, my eyes wide as I struggled not to respond aloud. Understanding dawned in the sphinx's eyes and he shook his head slightly before stepping close to me. "Let me help move you off her, little guy."

Harrison reared back in anger, his tongue flicking furiously. *"How dare he! Don't he know I'm the biggest snake around here? I'm no 'little guy'. I'll make his snake a little guy if he's not careful."*

I choked back an explosive giggle and turned it into a cough. Altan saw the humour written on my face. He couldn't hear the snake, but he must have put two and two together and realised the snake was not impressed with his word choice. "Sorry, Harry," he whispered. "You're a stunning specimen. But I do need you to slide off my colleague."

Grumbling, the carpet snake slithered down my arm and onto the floor before disappearing behind the feed bins. "Huh, that was weird. It's almost like he listened to you," Todd joked.

We both tittered nervously. Altan's warning to keep my strange powers to myself was ringing in my ears; there was no need to mention my ability to hear animals to the sanctuary's manager for now.

"Who else is on site today?" Altan asked smoothly, diverting the conversation.

"I know that Destiny is out right now. She'll be back to do her rounds later." At my confused expression, Todd added, "Destiny is our magica handler and always feeds out at morning and night time. She's out of mobile range for a few hours while she picks up more feed from one of our specialist providers. She'll be here after four o'clock, and again between eight and ten o'clock tomorrow morning." He checked his watch. "We should be able to find Clyde somewhere. If we don't come across him, I'll call him to meet us at the office."

A high-pitched voice interrupted us from the doorway. "You lookin' for me?"

As I spun around, I assumed I was looking at Clyde. The gnome was short and bore the usual leathery brown skin of his kind, but I had to admit I'd expected a gravelly voice rather than his squeaky one.

"Oh good, you're here," said Todd. "Clyde, these are the assessors from MagicAssess come to discuss the claim for the fire damage. Please answer their questions and give them access to any part of the sanctuary they request."

"Can do, mate," came the shrill response, followed by a hiccough. "Wotcha need from me right now? It's just that I need to fix the water kelpies' incubator again. It's been on the fritz since the fire and I gotta keep resetting it so the little tykes don't die before they hatch."

"We just need to know where you were at the time of the fire and if you noticed anything unusual," Altan said.

The gnome rubbed a hand over his chin and screwed up his face. He looked a bit like a wrinkled old potato that had been forgotten in the cupboard. "What day was that again?"

Altan raised his eyebrow at the gnome's apparent forgetfulness. "Last Tuesday."

"Erm... I might have been cleaning the pool that day in preparation for the hatchlings but I'd have to check me logs. I don't remember anythin' weird, but I'll be sure to let you know if I think of something."

"Please do." Altan's tone was firm. "Is there anyone you can think of who may have lit the fire on purpose? A disgruntled colleague? Maybe someone with a grudge against the sanctuary?"

The potato face was back as Clyde pursed his lips. "Ugh. It's too early in the morning to be pointin' fingers at people with no proof. Can't say I can think of any reason someone would set a fire."

"Fine. We'll call you if we have any other questions."

"Right-oh then," the gnome squeaked before trotting off in the direction of another much smaller shed. He stumbled a little before taking a swig from a hip flask.

As we returned to the sanctuary's office, I took down the contact details of the staff members. We promised Todd we'd be in touch soon and walked back slowly to Altan's car.

"All right. First impressions?" Altan prompted as soon as we'd fastened our seatbelts.

I took a deep breath as I gathered my thoughts. "It's looking like the fire was arson, probably via magical means... but why? Was it some random kids mucking around with a spell that took out the fence? Was the fence old and needing to be replaced, and Todd didn't want to fork out extra cash for the repairs so decided to give insurance fraud a go? Was the magical fire used to break the wards deliberately to gain access and steal something? But again, the question 'why' remains. Did they try to take something and fail? Or have they succeeded, and we still haven't figured out what they stole?"

"Good. Let's assume for a moment that the fire was purposely lit in order to gain access. Who could have done it?"

As we pulled up in front of the gate, I shrugged. "Anyone with magic or who is able to buy beads, so that doesn't tell us much." I got out and opened the gate, waited for Altan to drive through then shut it again.

Once I'd settled back in to my seat, Altan said, "Okay, let's go back to the 'why'."

I drummed my fingers against the car door as I thought. "Crime is usually committed because of love, revenge or money. I don't see how love could have anything to do with it."

"We have no real evidence, so we shouldn't dismiss anything at this stage. But for the sake of this argument, let's take love off the table. Revenge or money?"

"Todd seems like a lovely man, and I had no bad feelings about any of the staff. They're not out to make a profit, they're just trying to rehabilitate magicas. I don't see how revenge factors in. My gut is telling me it's because of money but the sanctuary doesn't carry any cash. To be honest, it kind of seems like they're broke."

"Which would point us back towards insurance fraud." Altan pulled onto the highway and headed north, back towards the Sunshine Coast.

"Well, yeah. But I didn't get a bad feeling about Todd. He seems genuine."

"Take your feelings out of it. We need to look at the evidence."

"But surely gut feelings have to come into it at some point?"

"That's how innocent people get sent to jail," Altan reprimanded me gently. "How many times have you heard stories about lawyers or the police making the evidence fit their theories? We want to find the truth."

I gave an impatient huff, frustrated by my own lack of experience. He reached over and squeezed my hand. "Don't be too hard on yourself. This is only your second claim. That's why I'm here with you. Between us we can gather evidence and figure this out. But running scenarios together as an exercise is good practice so you don't get stuck in a rut in your own head."

His touch was cool and it grounded me. The frazzled feeling dissipated as quickly as it had appeared, and I found myself automatically taking some calming breaths.

"Okay," I started slowly. "The facts. Todd is the owner of a run-down magica sanctuary that struggles to pay its bills on time. He is married to a satyr and has experienced prejudice about their relationship. There was a bushfire that appears to have been lit with magic. It breached the boundary fence and broke the fire wards. Today we met the vet who attended on the morning of the fire, along with her sister who is also her assistant. They seemed capable, although busy and therefore were abrupt with us. We also met Clyde, a gnome, who is the sanctuary's handyman and has a drinking problem. We didn't meet Destiny, the magica handler, but we'll contact her later today or tomorrow." I paused. "Did I miss anything?"

Altan flashed a cheeky smile as he overtook a caravan. "The fact that you got to cuddle a carpet python. What did he say to you?"

I shuddered as I recalled his coils hanging heavy on my shoulders. "He doesn't like the nickname Harry. He immediately corrected it to Harrison. And he'd already eaten some rats so wasn't interested in eating me." I didn't bother mentioning the snake's allusion to Altan's own...snake. Heat coloured my cheeks and I looked out the window so he didn't notice.

"Do you think we could ask Harrison about whether he saw anything that night?"

I buried my face in my hands. "Are you telling me I have to touch that snake again?"

Altan burst out laughing and I couldn't stop myself joining in. His laughter was infectious and I could have listened to it every day. Once his amusement had subsided, he said, "If it helps us solve the case then yes, that could be very useful." He regarded me for a moment before refocusing on the road. "Your talent seems to attract the most interesting choice in animals. First spiders, now snakes."

"And don't forget my tawny frogmouth friend."

He chuckled. "Yes, we can't forget about her. Have you spoken to her lately?"

"Not since I got back from Bowen." I stared pensively out the car window. "I wonder where she is."

"Trix..." the sphinx spoke my name slowly, his voice dragging over the x. A shiver raced up my spine and my heart squeezed; I could never get enough of hearing him say my name. I did my best to not reveal any hint of my feelings.

"What's up, Altan?" I asked casually. Too casually. Oh no: I was starting to attempt my own sensual voice, and it really didn't sound sexy. I was pretty sure I sounded like a bad actor in one of those adult films I definitely never watched on lonely nights. I should just shut my trap.

"I don't mean to pry but do you want to talk about your mother? I'm happy to be a listening ear if you need one." He studied me closely for a moment before returning his focus to the road.

It was like a bucket of ice had just been thrown over me and my flames of desire had been smothered as quickly as the firemen had taken care of the sanctuary's blaze. "Not really," I responded curtly.

He nodded and returned his focus to the business of navigating traffic.

I sighed. "Sorry. I don't mean to be rude. I do appreciate your offer, but she...gets under my skin. We always clash and she doesn't seem to recognise any of her problematic behaviour, either now or from when I was a kid. She wasn't really...present when I was little. I had to learn to take care of myself."

He frowned. "She neglected you?"

I opened my mouth to say no, but then I considered my childhood. I'd always called my mother scatterbrained, unsupportive and forgetful rather than neglectful, but I'd had to learn to cook for myself and make my own school lunches so that I didn't go hungry. She barely ever remembered to do laundry, so my bedsheets and towels only got washed when I did them. I only learnt that they should be washed regularly because of watching my friends' parents hanging out their linen. She never came to any school events or awards nights and I was constantly making excuses for her. Was that neglect? But to her credit, she always made sure there was food in the fridge, and she had never hurt me. She just wasn't good at looking after herself, let alone another, smaller, human.

"I'm not sure if I'd go as far as calling it neglect, but she's certainly never been very maternal. And now she's coming into my house for who knows how long. It puts me on edge."

A memory of Altan's history that he'd shared with me when we were in Bowen resurfaced. "I'm sorry, I'm being insensitive. I shouldn't be complaining – at least I still have my mother. I'm sorry you lost your parents."

"Don't apologise," he murmured. "I had my sister and a supportive adoptive family. Our experiences were different, and my loss doesn't negate yours." His lips curled into a smile, baring his canines. "If you need to escape her company, feel free to fake a work emergency. We can get started on the combat training that Barry suggested."

"Be careful, I might just take you up on that offer."

"Excellent. When did you say she was arriving?"

"I don't know exactly, but today sometime."

His amber eyes twinkled. "Perfect! So, Brazilian Jiu Jitsu training starts tonight, then?"

CHAPTER SIX

ONCE ALTAN HAD DROPPED me home and pulled away from the kerb, I rubbed my chest. Every time I said goodbye to him, the ache inside returned and deepened. He was a good friend and a wonderful mentor, but he was a work colleague and anything more would be inappropriate. I'd have to be very careful with my feelings.

Sighing at the loss of his company, I unlocked my house and looked at my messy living room and kitchen. I desperately needed to clean before my mother arrived.

One thing I was really enjoying about my new job was the relaxed hours. Sure, there would be days where I worked late, but it was nice to get dropped home early sometimes... although maybe not so nice today since I was hyper-focussed on my mother's impending arrival.

I wasn't certain I'd have time to go for a jog, but I worked up a sweat by racing around the house and cleaning as fast as I could.

I held onto a vague hope that if everything looked perfect, I could give my mother a good first impression and win her approval.

Was that something I should unpack with a therapist? Probably. I paused in the middle of my frenzied vacuuming. I finally had the money to book in for counselling so I should probably look into it. Shaking my head I decided I didn't have time right now.

While checking my phone constantly for updates, I threw a roast lamb along with potatoes, carrots and pumpkin into the oven, then scrubbed the kitchen bench. When there had been no new notifications after two hours, I tried calling my mother again. It went straight to voicemail.

Nicole and Millie arrived home at five-thirty. My best friend and now housemate had offered to pick up my daughter because the school team's netball practice finished at the same time that she'd be driving home. When I announced that my mother would be arriving at some point that evening, Nic promptly escaped to her room. Apparently, the mere mention of my mother had brought on a headache. I knew how she felt.

I decided to burn off some of my nervous energy and go for a jog. Asking Nic to keep an eye on the food in the oven and an ear out for the doorbell, I laced up my sneakers. Millie didn't join me because she was tired from netball, so I only went for an intense thirty-minute workout. I returned home sweating and still excessively anxious.

After a quick shower, I set the table, still checking my phone and the front window every few minutes. Finally, at six-thirty, the doorbell rang.

I opened the front door and there she was: my mother.

Although she was beautiful once, with her wild mane of brown hair, vibrant blue eyes, high-set cheekbones and naturally full lips, time hadn't been kind to her. But it wasn't age that had altered her appearance so much. Ever since I could remember,

Valerie had wandered through life in a kind of daze, her expression faraway and her worries never in the here and now.

Secretly I'd always been thankful to be an only child; at least I'd only had to parent myself and there had been no younger siblings for me to mother.

Val blinked her eyes slowly, as if surprised to see me open the door. I bared my teeth in an approximation of a smile. "Hey, Mum. Long time, no see."

"Hmmmm." She murmured an unintelligible greeting before snatching a lock of my dark hair that was hanging loose around my face. "You'd be so pretty if you cut it short." She looked me up and down. "And what have you been doing to your body?" She poked my right bicep and wrinkled her nose in distaste. "You're starting to look like a man."

I squeezed my eyes shut for a second and counted to five. She hadn't changed. "Come on in," I forced out and stepped aside.

Val looked around the house. "It's quite clean. You must have been busy this afternoon. It usually never looks this tidy."

Why had I said she could stay with me? I was sorely tempted to break out that griffin that had attacked me and set it on my mother.

"Nanna!" Millie squealed from the living room and launched herself off the couch.

My daughter was the only reason I still tolerated my mother's random visits; somehow, Val wasn't a completely useless grandmother.

"Hello, sweetheart." My mother wrapped her in a warm embrace and a familiar stirring of jealousy pooled in my gut. I scolded myself silently. No matter how much it stung, I refused to begrudge my daughter a positive relationship with her grandmother just because my feelings were hurt.

"When did you get here?" Millie asked breathlessly as she pulled back to look at my mother.

"Just flew in this morning. I was disappointed no one was waiting to meet me at the airport." She glanced over Millie's head at me.

"Well, Mum, if you'd replied to my text, call or email with the details of your flight, I would have happily figured out a way to pick you up."

She sniffed and looked away, ignoring my measured response to her passive-aggressive accusation. "I had to catch a bus all the way from Brisbane Airport! Do you know how much that costs?"

I gritted my teeth. "Would you like me to pay you back?"

She snorted. "Don't be silly, dear, I know you're always broke. To be honest, I'm surprised you've held onto this place. Your landlord must like charity cases." Another barb within five minutes of arriving. It was going to be a long visit.

"You probably didn't read the update in my email, but I actually have a new job. The pay is a lot better, so we're okay now."

Her head snapped back to me and her icy blue gaze pierced mine. "You quit? How could you do that to Fiona? That woman was a saint and looked after you for years. And you repaid her by jumping ship?" She shook her head in disgust. "There's no loyalty these days."

I really shouldn't let the woman get to me. I knew what she was like... but seriously?

"It was Fiona's idea for me to apply for the job," I all-but snarled. "Can't you just be happy for me for once?" Noticing Millie's slumped shoulders and downcast eyes, I took a steadying breath. Clearing my throat, I said, "I'm sure you're tired after travelling all day. You'll be taking Millie's bed, Mum, and she and I will share a room while you're here."

There was no way I would share a bedroom with my mother, and I'd never hear the end of it if I put her on the couch.

"Why aren't I in the spare room?"

"Nic moved in to help with rental costs so we don't have a spare room anymore. I mentioned it in my email."

Val looked around. "Is she home now?"

"Yep."

"So why hasn't she come out to greet me? That's very rude, you know. I was never allowed to hide in my room when we had guests."

"You realise Nic's not a child, right? And she's no relation to you? It really wouldn't matter if you didn't see her at all while you're here."

Millie cleared her throat. "How long are you staying with us, Nanna?"

My mother shot me a scowl before turning to her. "I'm not sure, sweetheart. It will depend on a few things. Maybe a few days, maybe a few weeks. We'll see."

I nearly choked on my spit. No way could I deal with her for a few weeks! It was time to change the subject before I lashed out. "Why don't you go and freshen up, Mum? I left a clean towel and facecloth on Millie's bed for you. While you're doing that, I'll get dinner dished up."

She opened her mouth as if to continue her verbal attack but thought better of it and gave a curt nod when she saw Millie's expression. Once she'd disappeared into my daughter's bedroom, I breathed a long sigh of relief.

"Mum," Millie asked as she gathered utensils from the drawer, "why do you and Nanna fight so much?"

"I'm sorry you had to see that. It's a long story and not one I want to share tonight."

She gave a hesitant nod but looked dissatisfied as she set the table. It was time for me to change the subject. "How was school today? And netball practice? You were training with your new team, right?"

She puffed out her chest, so proud of herself for getting accepted onto the seniors' team and launched into a play-by-play of which drills they'd done and what the older girls had said to her. I listened happily, pleased to know that even though she was two years younger than the oldest player, they were impressed enough by her ability and work ethic to include her.

Nic snuck out, quickly grabbed a plate of dinner and disappeared back into her room to eat alone.

My mother came out smelling of my body wash and sat at the head of the dining table. I joined her as Millie excitedly repeated her story for her beloved grandmother. I tuned out and kept my eyes on my food until Millie asked, "So what have you been doing Nanna? We haven't seen you since last Christmas. Have you been travelling?"

I couldn't be sure, but I was almost certain that Valerie froze for a split second. She was always evasive whenever I asked what she did during the months she disappeared. Was it a sex thing? Did she have a toy boy? Did she go on religious sabbaticals? Volunteer in a third-world country? Or was she slumming it for months at a time and only visiting when she couldn't stand sleeping on the streets for another night? I didn't have a clue.

I eyed her cautiously and wondered if I'd have to interrupt her story if it was only appropriate for adult ears.

"Just a bit of this and that," she replied airily. "Lots of travelling and learning. It's been extremely enlightening. I'll have to take you on a trip one day, sweetheart. Wouldn't that be nice? If you could go anywhere in the world, where would you like to go?" she asked, effectively distracting Millie who launched into a monologue about all the things she loved about Europe.

It wasn't until we were clearing the table that my mother finally asked about me. As I poured detergent into the sink, she sidled up with her plate and glass and sighed. "So tell me about this new job that's giving you all this money."

I scowled at the bubbles in the sink and started aggressively scrubbing the roasting pan. If there ever was a reason for me to break my no swearing rule, Val was that reason.

Before I could respond, Millie bounced up with her own dirty plate and stated, "Mum found the Big Mango last month! She flew to Bowen in North Queensland with her new boss to check whether the owner was lying and trying to commit insurance fraud. But he was a good guy in the end, and it was his worker who had a crush on him that had spelled it invisible to get his attention! And this worker had a spider weaver attack Mum, but Mum fought him off. She caught the bad guy – or woman, technically – and saved the day! It sounded like a movie!"

I smiled at my daughter's interpretation of the events of my first claim. I *sounded* badass, though I certainly didn't feel it.

My mother raised her eyebrows and looked at me in surprise. "Really?"

"Hard to believe but yes, I was competent in my new job," I grumbled.

"Don't get your knickers in a twist." Val turned away from me in a huff. Maybe I should call Altan now to come get me for that late-night combat training session he'd mentioned.

A sharp tap-tap-tap at the window interrupted our bickering. "What is that?" my mother screeched, holding her hands to her cheeks as she stared out the window at Froggy.

I glared at her. "No need to get your knickers in a twist," I fed her own words back to her. It was petty but worth it. "It's a tawny frogmouth. She visits our yard sometimes."

"So cute!" Millie gazed at the bird in adoration.

"I like your daughter," said Froggy. She cocked her head towards my mother. *"Not her so much."*

I rolled my eyes. "Couldn't agree more," I muttered.

Valerie narrowed her eyes as she looked between me and the bird. "What did you say?"

I gave a guilty start. "Nothing," I replied hurriedly, but I could feel the heat creeping up my face. I was a terrible liar.

"What a cool noise!" Millie exclaimed. "I've never heard a tawny frogmouth's call before. Hey, little baby, you okay?" she cooed. Froggy cocked her head and sidled closer.

"She's an adult," I quickly corrected. "I've been calling her Froggy."

My mother frowned and stared at the bird. "What an...odd name," she murmured and pinched the bridge of her nose. Suddenly glaring at the tawny frogmouth, she flicked her hands in a shooing motion. "Scram! Don't let it mark the windowsill's paint."

"Hey!" I exclaimed as Froggy flew away. "You scared her!"

"It's just a wild bird," she muttered. Rubbing her head, she announced abruptly, "I'm going to bed. Make sure you don't wake me before seven otherwise I'll be out of sorts for the rest of the day."

I raised my eyebrows but returned my eyes to the sink and said nothing. If this was her *in* sorts, there was no way I wanted to see her out of them.

Chapter Seven

The day felt like it was stretching on forever. And it wasn't over yet.

After finishing the dishes, I grabbed my phone and went to my bedroom where I reluctantly pulled up my ex's number. He and Millie were in contact most weeks via video call, but she usually spoke to him in her room. My finger hovered over the call button. It wasn't that I hated Chris or couldn't stand speaking to him, but he'd let me know how he felt about me many years ago, and I'd come to realise that it was for the best.

We hadn't been on the same page and we wanted very different things out of life. At the time, I'd have given up all my dreams for him if he'd asked me to, but I would have been miserable. I'd already felt some resentment creeping in but had squashed it down, telling myself that marriage was meant to be about self-sacrifice and compromise. Although maybe not when only one of the partners was doing all the compromising.

We had remained amicable but that didn't mean we were friends. Most weeks he remembered to transfer a small amount of money into my bank account towards Millie's school expenses. Whenever there was a bigger bill, such as a school camp, I'd let him know and if he had the money he'd transfer half. It had worked for us for close to nine years, but I still felt weird about calling to ask for money.

I huffed a sigh and pressed the call button.

"Hey Trix, this is a surprise. Is Millie okay?" His ocker accent was growing stronger with every passing year.

"Yes, yes, Millie is fine," I assured him. "How're you, Chris?"

"Flat out with work but it's great!" His boyish enthusiasm hadn't changed. "Laney and I have been in Tassie investigating a magica-smuggling ring. It's been insane! Should have an article published on it next month."

"Oh, goodness. That's...crazy. I'll tell Millie to keep her eyes peeled for it." There was an awkward pause. I noticed he hadn't bothered to ask how I was.

"Sorry to rush you, Trix, but I'm heading out the door. Why are you calling?"

"Oh, sorry. I was just calling to let you know that Millie got accepted as a reserve for the senior netball team at school and she's off to state in a few weeks. She might not get to play, but she still needs a uniform and new shoes as well as the cost of accommodation and the bus to Brisbane."

There was silence on the other end of the line.

May as well rip the plaster off while I was on a roll. "She's also been invited to a week-long performing arts workshop in October. Her heart is absolutely set on going. I'm going to apply for a grant, but if she doesn't get it I'm not sure I can afford the workshop on top of the netball expenses. Is there any chance you could chip in?"

"Yeah..." His sounded strained. "I should be able to put something towards it. Send me a text with the total amount and I'll see what I can afford."

"Okay, sounds good. Thanks, Chris." I kept my own voice light, even though I felt frustrated. He wasn't the one paying for all Millie's food and the fuel to take her to these events. He had his girlfriend Laney, and they didn't have kids. It wasn't like he was the one struggling to make ends meet.

"No worries. See you, Trix. Give my love to Millie, will you?"

Before I could respond, he'd hung up. Scowling, I chucked my phone on the bed beside me. While I was feeling miffed, I decided I might as well make a start on that grant application and get all the bad stuff over with in one day. Tomorrow would seem amazing in comparison.

I opened my laptop and found the email from Mrs Snow with the details of the workshop and grant followed by the link to the website and read through the guidelines. It was basically a scholarship. If Millie's application was accepted, she would receive seventy-five percent of the cost of her chosen workshop from the local council. That would be a big help; just because I was now earning a better wage didn't mean I wouldn't try and save money where I could. And if the council wanted to give my girl money to chase her dreams, I wouldn't say no.

I settled back against my pillow, created an account on the website and started typing. The first part of the application was simple and asked questions about Millie's background and the workshop she would attend if she was successful. Then they asked for my income and asset details and I winced. I understood that they needed to assess the applicants, but it still felt invasive. Reluctantly, I answered the rest of the questions and submitted the form.

Logging off, I took my laptop to my dresser and plugged it into the socket to charge overnight. I stretched while I was standing as

I could already feel my muscles complaining after this morning's time in the battle chamber. I knew it would be worse tomorrow. I'd need to do some stretches in the morning to improve my recovery time.

Returning to my bed, I sat down on the edge of it and opened the drawer in the bedside table. Ignoring the pink vibrator that was tucked against the side, I looked at my stick, the one I'd yanked out of the komada dragon's mouth. It looked completely innocuous but I couldn't help wondering about its magical properties. There was no doubt in my mind that it wasn't a normal stick, and I was almost certain that the only reason I'd survived the spider weaver's attack was because of its help.

Pulling it out, I ran my fingers over the smooth timber and noted the little knot in one end. A surge of warmth spread through my fingers, as if it was happy to greet me. With a quiet squeak, I dropped it on the bed and held my hand over my heart. "Honestly, I shouldn't even be surprised anymore," I muttered.

I picked it up again but held on this time when it pulsed with energy. "What am I supposed to do with you, huh?"

The stick didn't respond. I groaned with frustration and put it back in the drawer.

I stared pensively at the wall. I knew I had to figure out what the deal was with that stick, but in the meantime I should probably keep reading the tome that I'd borrowed from the library. It promised to share everything there was to know about avian magicas. I was halfway through it, and it *was* extremely interesting, but I had to admit it was a hard slog after a long day at work plus parenting. Not to mention the unwelcome arrival of my mother.

With a sigh, I picked it up – and promptly dropped it when my phone pinged with an incoming text. I abandoned the book and grabbed my phone. That was the good thing about books: they'd still be waiting patiently once you'd finished being distracted by everything else.

Dear Trix, I am writing to say that I was impressed with your work today. I am very pleased with your progress. I hope you feel proud of yourself and all that you have achieved in a short time. Sincerely yours, Altan.

My chest ballooned at the warm compliments. I grinned both at the formality of his text and the fact he was texting at all.

Hey Altan, thanks for the message. I'm trying my best and learning lots, I'm just glad you think I'm doing a good job. Also, I've already saved your number to my phone so you don't need to sign off your texts.

He replied quickly.

Dear Trix, is it not good manners to greet the recipient and sign-off in business correspondence? Sincerely yours, Altan.

In text form, no. You just sound old.

I am not old.

I sniggered.

There you go, you're getting it now. Good job.

I was staring at the screen with a goofy smile, waiting for another ping, when my door swung open, and Millie wandered in already dressed in her pyjamas. Locking my phone, I shifted my focus to her. "Hey, little dove. How're you tonight?"

"Pretty good. I've got a music assignment due on Friday, and another one for English that's due next week that's stressing me out. Also, before I forget, I need you to sign a permission slip for school. I need to take a gold coin donation on Thursday for free dress day, and I need you to pay for the excursion next month. Oh, and I also need money for tuckshop tomorrow because there's no food in the fridge."

I laughed. "Really? There's no food in the fridge at all?"

"Well," she blustered, "there is, but none of it is what I usually have in my lunchbox." She hesitated, worrying her lip. "You told me last week that your new job pays well and that we could afford for me to get tuckshop sometimes. Is that still okay?"

"Yes, Millie, it's fine. Thank you for checking, but we're good now. Remind me in the morning and I'll sign your permission slip and get your tuckshop money and a one-dollar coin for your donation." I stifled a yawn. "I'm exhausted. And tomorrow will be another big day. Time for bed, love."

She bent down and gave me a goodnight hug, then crawled into bed beside me. Fluffing up the spare pillow, she tucked her amber hair behind her ears and settled in.

Looking at her for a long moment before I turned off the light, I flashed back to the difficult months of us being alone after Chris had left. Millie and I had often shared a bed then and I'd found solace in the sound of her steady breathing beside me. It had been a few years since she'd snuck in for cuddles and I'd grown used to the silence, but it was both comforting and nostalgic to hear her soft breaths as she fell asleep.

My little girl might be growing up, but she could come back to me for snuggles anytime.

I checked my phone one last time and my heart fell a little when I saw there was no response from Altan. I hoped I hadn't offended him. I debated sending him a goodnight text but quickly dismissed the idea. That would be a slippery slope into blurring the lines of our working relationship.

My life was complicated enough without adding an office romance to it.

CHAPTER EIGHT

I WAS DRESSED IN my armour and waiting for Altan at the end of my driveway at eight o'clock sharp. I'd already spent a long time stretching my stiff muscles that morning and even managed a gentle jog around my neighbourhood to loosen up. Once I'd returned home, I'd watered my succulent named Heather in her pretty purple pot, showered, done a load of washing, and then eaten breakfast with Millie and Nic before Val had even woken up.

Millie had caught the bus to school and Nic had left for the office early, claiming she had extra insurance broking training. Somehow I doubted that, but I didn't begrudge her the need to escape. Before I'd managed to get out of the house, my mother had already complained about the discomfort of Millie's bed, the distant noise of traffic, the streetlight she claimed was shining in her eyes all night even through the blinds, the lack of variety in our breakfast choices, and about my work attire. I was tired already and the day hadn't even begun. I had no idea what she was planning on doing that day – and I found that I didn't really care.

Altan pulled up in his black sedan. Time to find out if he was mad with me. A whiff of sandalwood and leather hit me as I opened the passenger door. Sliding into the seat, I asked, "All righty, tell me straight. Are you upset with me?"

He shot me a confused look. "What? No! Why?"

"You didn't reply to my message last night. And because my last message was a tease, and sometimes jokes get lost in translation when delivered over text message, I was worried that I'd offended you." Searching his face, I found nothing to worry about.

"Your last message made me laugh but I didn't have anything further to say. I figured you were going to bed, so I thought I'd leave you alone."

I blinked. "Oh."

He chuckled. "There's no need to overthink it, Trix. I'm sorry if I worried you. I must admit I'm a little hazy on text etiquette. How would you like me to respond in future?"

"It's up to you. But usually if a text makes me laugh, I reply with a 'ha ha', or a laughing emoji. Or something."

Altan stared at me. "You literally want me to write the words, 'ha ha'?"

When he put it like that, it did sound ridiculous. "You don't have to," I mumbled. Clearing my throat, I decided a change of subject was in order. "So, where are we off to today?" I asked, rubbing my hands together.

"Where do you think we should go?"

"Back to the sanctuary?"

"Don't *ask* me, *tell* me. You need practice taking the lead for when I'm busy handling a different claim. You'll be on your own soon enough."

A pang of sadness lanced my heart, but I ignored it. That was another reason one shouldn't get involved with one's colleagues: it was far too distracting when there was work to be done.

"Okay," I started. "Todd told us that Destiny would be at the sanctuary between eight and ten today so we'll go chat to her, then we'll head to the police station and talk to the officers who attended on the day. We need to get their reports: both official and anything off the record."

"Sounds as good a plan as I could have come up with," he said with a proud smile.

Warmth filled my insides, and I looked out the window to hide my delight. "Do we know who we're talking to at the police station?"

"Sergeant Barracks is the name on the report."

I brightened. "Oh, that's okay then."

"Do you know him?" Altan asked.

"Not personally, but I've heard his name mentioned by an old magica client of mine. Apparently, he did help them find a thief. Barracks seems less inclined to be a jerk towards magicas."

Altan pursed his lips. "Well, we saw how the officers up north handled the last claim when the property owner was an elf. It will be interesting to see the difference. I hope your information is correct."

At that moment I shocked both of us by yelling, "Stop the car!"

"Shit!" Altan jolted in his seat but swiftly pulled in to the side of the road. "What's wrong?" he asked, but I'd already leapt out of the vehicle before he'd pulled on the handbrake.

I jogged back to the street sign that had caught my eye on the corner of the quiet intersection and put my hands on my hips. "Did you want me?" I asked the tawny frogmouth that was eyeing me.

"It's actually you who wants me," Froggy replied smugly.

"Fantastic." I paused. "What precisely do you mean by that?"

Altan joined me and looked between the bird and me. He tapped three fingers against his chest and raised them in the magica greeting salute. "It is my pleasure to meet you. I am Altan. I assume you must be Froggy." Froggy bowed her head in greeting. "What's going on?"

"Great question," I retorted. When he raised a questioning eyebrow, I added, "She's being deliberately obtuse."

Eyes crinkling, Altan's amusement grew as he studied the tawny frogmouth. "I see."

I held up a finger to quieten him as Froggy ruffled her grey and brown feathers and sighed. *"You're no fun. I can't see everything, you know. I just had a premonition that you would require my assistance today, so here I am. At your service,"* she added sarcastically.

Turning to Altan, I explained, "She wants to come with us to the sanctuary. Can I say why?" I glanced at Froggy for permission in case her talent for seeing the future was a secret. When she bobbed her head, I continued, "She had a premonition that we'd need her today."

"She has premonitions? That's interesting. Who am I to argue with a bird? Come on, let's get going."

Froggy flew from the street sign to the roof of his car. *"I'm ready."*

I stared at her. "You can't travel on the car roof!"

She shot me a haughty glare. *"And why not?"*

Altan's face had grown pale at the sight of Froggy's talons scratching the roof of his car. "Because you'll give him a coronary if you continue to mark his baby."

Froggy turned her head from side to side in confusion. *"His baby? He has offspring? I do not see the child."*

I couldn't help myself. I burst out laughing.

"It's not funny," Altan said with a pained whine to his voice.

"Froggy." I did my best to control my chuckles. "Please get off Altan's car and on to my arm. I am calling the car his baby because he looks after it. It is not actually his child. Regardless, you can't ride on the roof because we'll be driving too fast and you'll be blown away. You'll have to travel inside the car."

She gave an irritated fluff of her wings. *"I don't like being inside."*

I shrugged. "Well, it's either that or you don't come. Or you could fly there yourself, but I imagine that would take you a day or two."

She sighed irritably. *"Fine. I'll travel with you inside the metal death trap."* She flew on to my shoulder and gripped tightly. It was fortunate I was wearing my armour because I didn't feel anything worse than pressure from her claws.

Traffic was heavy but not at a standstill, for which I was thankful. Froggy stayed silent for the entire car ride, clinging to my shoulder and hiding her head under my ponytail. Meanwhile Altan and I went back over the facts of the claim and then our suspect list. It wasn't very long or had any solid reasoning behind it, but it was good practice.

When we pulled into the sanctuary carpark, we still hadn't made any headway on who the fire starter might be. As we got out, Froggy immediately took flight to the closest tree as I glanced around at the other cars. The red hatchback and the white ute were still there, together with two new additions: a silver sedan parked discreetly beside the ute, and a glaringly bright orange sports car parked across two spaces in front of the entrance to the donga.

I raised an eyebrow and glanced at Altan. "I wonder who that belongs to."

We headed towards the office where raised voices greeted us. Altan murmured, "I think we're about to find out."

I placed my hand on the doorknob and hesitated when I heard Todd's softer voice saying, "I'm sorry, but we've already committed to donating it to the university."

There was muffled spluttering then a male voice that I didn't recognise replied, "The university? How could you? Science experiments on such a beautiful creature... it's not right!" He sounded English and very posh.

"Whoever it is, he's mad as a cut snake," I muttered to Altan.

"Mad as a what?" He shook his head. "You Australians really do have the most colourful language."

I flashed him a grin. As we opened the door, I saw that Todd was looking even more tired than usual. He was raking his hands through his strawberry-blond hair, making it look particularly unkempt. "You are only going to stuff it and put it on display. I really don't see what the difference is," he said with a frustrated sigh.

"Such beauty should be conserved," the man retorted.

"At least this way the life wasn't lost in vain," Todd argued. "The university can utilise the unicorn's properties."

More pompous spluttering followed. "You mean hack it up into little bits and sell it to the highest bidder?"

"The uni has had great success in discovering new medical treatments with magical properties, but they're lacking in ethically sourced ingredients. We can help. I'm sorry, Reginald, but this is what's happening."

"I can't believe it! Don't my feelings matter to you at all? You know how much money I've donated to this place. My generosity is the only reason the sanctuary is still functioning. I'd have thought you'd want to keep me happy."

I glanced at Altan; that sounded almost like a threat.

"Don't be like that," Todd replied. "I do my best to keep you happy, but when it comes down to saving lives versus maintaining the integrity of a dead body for display purposes, I know which I have to choose. I don't owe you anything."

Both men noticed us at the same time and the scowl on the stranger's face immediately lifted at the sight of an audience. "Good morning, and who do we have here?" The Englishman beamed at us as he flicked an imaginary speck of dust off his aubergine suit. How the heck could he wear a suit in this weather?

I was already heating up in my armour and it wasn't even summer yet.

"This is Trix and Altan from MagicAssess," Todd explained. "They're here to discuss the insurance claim for the fire damage. This is Lord Reginald Chatsworth, one of MSQ's loyal patrons."

His lordship's smile faltered but he recovered quickly and shook both our hands. "So pleased to meet you both. I'm desperately sorry, but I must dash. Good luck with sorting out the claim. I hope you'll ensure it is paid out promptly; Todd needs a little less stress in his life." He clapped Todd on the shoulder before giving a jaunty salute with his cane and swiftly making his way outside in the direction of the orange sports car.

We shared a look as he roared out of the carpark then Altan cleared his throat and asked, "What's this about a dead body?"

CHAPTER NINE

Todd chuckled nervously. "It sounds bad when you put it like that. Unfortunately, we lost one of the unicorns yesterday afternoon." The grief was evident in his voice. "To lose an adult unicorn on top of the slipped foal...it's heartbreaking for all of us. Unicorns are notoriously difficult to save once illness or infection takes hold of their bodies. They can seem fine one day and fade fast when no one's looking. I suppose it's a blessing that he didn't suffer long, but it still hurts every time I lose a magica."

"So it wasn't the foal's mother that passed?" I asked.

"No. The mare is still unwell, but it was the stallion that we lost yesterday."

"When did he come into care?"

"Two weeks ago. A member of the public had found him acting lethargic in some bushlands nearby. We had Anna, the vet, check him over and he had a slight temperature. We were giving him antibiotics, and Destiny and I were taking turns to check on him every few hours. He seemed to have stabilised, but sadly he died yesterday."

"I'm sorry to hear that," I murmured. "That must be hard."

"It is, but death is a part of the job. You need to have a thick skin around here."

"So I take it that Lord Chatsworth was hoping you would give him the body?" Altan asked.

Todd twisted his wedding band around his finger. "Ah, you heard all of that. Yes, Reginald likes to collect magical artifacts for his personal exhibit as well as magica properties that can be used in rare beads or potions. He's constantly on the lookout for anything magical that he can get his hands on. The idea of having an entire unicorn body to display had him weak at the knees, but it's not the best or most ethical use of the remains."

I typed furiously on the tablet as Altan pressed him further. "What do you mean when you say anything 'he can get his hands on'? Are you suggesting he deals in black-market goods?"

Todd froze. "I've only heard rumours," he stammered. "I don't know anything for certain, so I'm not going to spread idle gossip. Especially not about the sanctuary's most generous patron."

"If you know something, Todd, we'd appreciate any information you can divulge."

"I know nothing," he replied stubbornly and crossed his arms.

Altan gave a frustrated sigh. "Fine, but if you do hear anything more than idle gossip, please keep us in the loop."

"You betcha." Todd pasted on a fake smile.

I was fairly sure he was lying to protect his patron but at that point I didn't think it was particularly important.

Altan raised an eyebrow. "We will need his phone number."

Todd looked reluctant. "Fine, but please don't upset him."

"We'll do our best." I gave him a reassuring smile as I slid the tablet into my bag and snapped the clasp shut. "Right now, though, we're here to see Destiny." Maybe a change of subject would ease the sudden tension in the room.

"Certainly!" Todd sounded relieved. "She's at the griffin enclosure."

Of course she was. I crossed my fingers behind my back, hoping the griffin wasn't in the mood to attack today.

Todd left us to find our own way to the griffin enclosure while he stayed in the office. As we walked down the wide path listening to the cackle of a kookaburra, I said, "Hey! Hey, Altan." I waggled my eyebrows. "Guess what?"

"What?" he asked, a smile already teasing his lips in response to the humour in my voice.

"We've got...wait for it...a date with Destiny!" I added some dramatic flair to her name.

He stopped walking and stared at me in mock horror. "Do you know, I think your puns might be worse than Barry's, and that's saying something." He shook his head and chuckled.

Our laughter was interrupted by high-pitched shrieks and I shot Altan a look. Once again we drew our weapons before we arrived at the griffin's enclosure but as we ran forward, a woman yelled at us, "You can put those away!"

We slowed and looked around for the speaker. A woman in her twenties was inside the enclosure throwing whole fish to the griffin who was shrieking with excitement at the prospect of food. Her bright-blue hair made it easy to locate her. "I'll be with you in a sec!" she called over her shoulder.

We waited patiently for her to come out of the pen. As soon as she'd emptied the bucket of fish, she took off her gloves and threw them in the empty bucket. Walking to the boundary, she pressed her hand to a blue crystal in the trunk of a tree. There was a shimmering in the air in front of her then the foliage parted to create a gap in the natural barrier. She quickly stepped through, and thick vines grew over the space once more.

As she joined us, the wild griffin finished off the last of his fish and half-loped, half-flew towards us. I eyed him distrustfully, my hand resting against the hilt of my sword, ready to grab if necessary.

As he drew level with me, the griffin made a strange clicking noise with his beak and stared at me intently. "Hey, mate," I said slowly. "Sorry about last month. I hope it's healing okay."

He shoved his face as close as he could to the foliage that separated us, and I took a cautious step back. The griffin clacked his beak again; he seemed irritated.

"Huh. I've never seen him act like that before," Destiny mused. "Hi! Todd told me you'd be coming for a chat today. I'm Destiny. I take care of the day-to-day needs of the sanctuary's magicas." She shook our hands.

The griffin's stare was still unnerving me, but I tried to put him out of my thoughts so I could focus on Destiny. After we'd introduced ourselves, I explained that we were interviewing all the sanctuary's employees to try and figure out who had caused the fire.

She told us the same story as everyone else. She'd arrived that morning for work to find the police cars and fire trucks filling the car park. She hadn't noticed anything out of the ordinary and didn't know how the fire had started. After she'd given her statement to the police officer, she'd helped Anna before starting her usual feeding routine with the magicas in her care. When she'd finished, she'd assisted Clyde with preparing the saltwater pool for the water kelpies.

"And how is everything going with the sanctuary?" Altan asked.

She frowned and tucked a wayward strand of blue hair behind her ear. "What do you mean?"

"Is money tight? Do you get paid on time? Are repairs to the sanctuary attended to in a timely manner?"

Putting her hands on her hips, Destiny asked, "What does that have to do with anything?"

Altan mimicked her posture. "Allow me to be blunt. Does Todd seem like he might have caused the fire to claim the insurance money?"

Destiny snorted. "No way. Todd is the most honest guy I've ever met. He'd never risk hurting his beloved magicas."

"Do you know anything about Lord Chatsworth?" I asked, hoping she might be more forthcoming with information than Todd had been.

She snapped her mouth shut and stared at us. Finally she said in a clipped tone, "He is a valued patron of the sanctuary."

"We heard a rumour, and we're just trying to ascertain if he was involved in the fire in any way," I wasn't exactly lying, though I'd admit I was stretching the truth a little. "Has he ever asked you to steal anything from a magica?"

"Why would you even ask that?" She folded her arms defensively. "I'm not the old man's servant, I just do my job and get out of here. I don't do illegal shit for nobody."

I wondered if she knew she'd used a double negative; maybe she was trying not to lie and was excellent at wordplay. I wouldn't have put that past her if she'd been a vampire since they tended to have carefully worded contracts with their blood volunteers. Of course, Destiny was only a human so perhaps not.

Altan pressed her. "You're not actually answering our questions. Has Lord Chatsworth ever asked you to steal for him?"

"No," she replied coldly.

"Do you have any idea who might have started the fire or why?"

"No," she repeated.

The griffin threw itself at the barrier and screamed loudly. I clapped my hands over my ears at the burst of sound. Destiny looked at him and frowned before returning her gaze to us. "He doesn't like you. Please leave before he hurts himself." She turned on her heel and stalked away, effectively ending the conversation.

"Rude," I whispered, but walked away from the enclosure anyway. The griffin's shrieks followed us until we were out of sight.

With the tablet balanced in one hand, I quickly wrote some notes before locking it and returning it to my bag. I tapped my chin as a thought occurred to me. "Altan, I want to check something."

He bowed and said simply, "I shall follow your lead."

I walked past the office, through the carpark then around the outside of the sanctuary, following the boundary until we found the broken section of the fence. In front of it, black grass stretched out in an unnaturally straight line. "Todd was right," I said and pointed at the charred grass. "That's weird, right?"

The sphinx nodded. "Very odd indeed. Magic wasn't *only* used to break the fence. Even the path of the fire was magical in nature. The arsonist planned this carefully and left nothing to chance. They wanted the fire to burn in this direction to break the fence here. But, once again, we're left with the question *why?*"

I walked along the path of dead grass, studying the extent of the damage as I went. Small tufts of green were already pushing through the earth. A faint charcoal smell lingered but it wasn't strong as it had been almost a week since the day of the fire.

We followed the black trail into a small forested area where the larger trees hadn't burned to the ground and picked our way carefully through the surviving undergrowth. Aside from feeling a touch warm, I was relieved my armour was comfortable and I'd thought to wear sneakers.

Spiky bushes with charred leaves impeded our progress until eventually, we couldn't get any further.

"I told you that you would need my assistance," Froggy's voice popped into my head, and I yelped.

"What's wrong?" Altan was already drawing his sword and looking for danger.

"Nothing. Froggy surprised me, that's all." I held my hand to my chest as I tried to slow my heart rate.

"Calm down. I simply wanted you to know I can fly into places where you can't walk. There was no need to jump like a joey."

Scanning the trees near me, I asked, "Where are you?"

"Right here."

I studied each limb of the closest gum tree, then shook my head. "Nope, still can't find you." The branch closest to my face moved and I bit back another squeal.

"Your camouflage abilities are impressive," Altan told the bird.

"Thanks," she replied with a happy fluff of her feathers.

"She said 'thanks'," I translated. "And she wants us to know she can fly into that thicket to see where the fire originated."

"Fantastic." He addressed the tawny frogmouth. "We would be very grateful for your assistance."

"I like him. He has manners." Froggy flew away and disappeared before I could respond.

I turned to Altan. "The fire must have travelled fast, otherwise more of the established trees and bushes would have been destroyed."

He nodded slowly. "That's a good point. Make sure you note that in the file once we're out of here."

"No worries. And I want to know your thoughts about something else: Destiny. She seemed—"

"Fractious? Suspicious? Rude?" he supplied.

I chuckled. "All of the above." I sobered and shifted my weight. "It's not like we're actually accusing her of anything yet, we just need some answers so we can rule her out as a suspect. Doesn't she understand that?"

"I'm not sure that she does. She wouldn't be the first innocent person I've questioned who has acted suspiciously. It makes them uncomfortable and often gets their backs up, so they stop answering. The more claims you assess, the more you'll see it."

He stopped talking when Froggy flew back and landed near his head. "What do you have to report, Froggy?" Altan asked before looking to me to translate.

"Not much, unfortunately. It's been almost a week so there's not much left to see. There were no tyre tracks or footprints that I could see either in or out of this bushland. I located the starting point of the fire, but it was just a big black starburst on the ground."

I repeated what Froggy had said to Altan. "So that tells us that the fire was definitely lit by magical means." He sounded thoughtful. "A black starburst also tells us that it was lit using a spell, not a bead or a fire-breathing magica."

"He can figure all that out by me telling him about a black starburst on the ground?" Froggy fixed me with a beady glare. *"So he's polite and intelligent. What are you waiting for, Trix?"*

I blushed deeply and was tempted to throw some ash at her face to shut her up. Fortunately Altan didn't seem to notice anything. "Come on, ladies, let's head back to the car."

Froggy flew to my shoulder and grabbed on tightly once more. It was going to be a long drive back to the Sunshine Coast.

Chapter Ten

We let Froggy out of the car a couple of blocks before the Maroochydore Police Station so she could fly back to my home.

The building was a concrete monstrosity with a few spindly-looking shrubs out the front. It wasn't exactly welcoming. Altan and I strode up to the glass front doors, and I shivered as we entered. The lino flooring squeaked as we walked towards the front desk where a young policewoman was sitting behind a glass partition looking at a computer.

She glanced at us and her eyes narrowed when she noticed Altan's cat-like ears. "Good morning. Please take a ticket and I'll be with you shortly." She spoke sternly and kept her eyes trained on her computer screen, refusing to meet Altan's gaze.

I looked around the room and pursed my lips. We were the only people waiting. "Why do we need a ticket when there's no one else here?" I asked.

Her mouth thinned. "It's protocol," she snapped. "Please take a ticket." She waved her hand towards a small machine to our left.

Altan rolled his eyes, took a ticket and stepped away from the counter. "I'm not in the mood to argue about the pointlessness of protocol this morning," he muttered to me.

We didn't bother to sit on the stained couch against the wall. Instead, Altan opted to stand in the middle of the room, facing the seated officer, where he proceeded to fold his arms and stare her down. He stayed in that position until the woman behind the glass gave a frustrated huff and called our number.

We approached the desk again and Altan introduced us. "We'd like to speak to the officer in charge of the fire damage case at the Magica Sanctuary of Queensland," he said politely.

"Which fire? Do you realise how many incidents we have to respond to? You can't just expect me to know what you're talking about. I need the police report number."

"If you are ready, I have the police report number right here," he replied calmly – a little too calmly. I could feel his frustration boiling beneath the surface.

She glared at him. Her hands hovered over the keyboard as she waited for him to recite the numbers. Before he could begin, a male uniformed police officer appeared behind the counter.

He smiled at us warmly. "Sorry, I thought I heard you say something about the sanctuary fire? I'm Sergeant Steven Barracks, the officer in charge of that incident. Where are you from?"

We showed him our MagicAssess identification cards.

"Oh, wonderful! Please, join me in the conference room." He placed his hand on the woman's shoulder. "I've got it from here."

She scowled as Barracks took us to another room. If I'd been a more childish person, I would have given her a cheeky wave. It was a good thing I was a mature, professional adult.

I tried hard not to look, but it was difficult not to notice how snugly the uniform fit the officer's muscled body. He appeared to be in his late thirties, clean-shaven, blond haired ¬– and he obviously worked out. I knew a lot of women who loved a man in uniform. Nicole would have had a fit if she'd been there.

The room he took us to was white and bright, with a grey couch and a couple of armchairs next to a pale wooden coffee table. There was a water cooler and a green plant in the corner that looked lovely… until I did a double take and realised it was plastic.

"Can I get you guys anything? Water, coffee, tea? I'm afraid I don't have any biscuits or cake. I'm trying to watch my figure, you know?" He chuckled and patted his non-existent belly.

Altan shook his head. "We're fine, thank you. We just wanted to discuss the fire at the sanctuary. We're investigating the claim and have some concerns."

Barracks waved at the couch as he settled in one of the armchairs facing it. "Take a seat. What concerns do you have, and how can I help?"

"From the written report our office received from you, it appears that the police and fire departments ruled it as a bushfire, not arson and not theft. We believe that conclusion was wrong."

Barracks ran his fingers through his hair, ruffling the wavy locks and making himself look even more magazine-cover ready. "Well, you certainly don't mince your words. That's quite an accusation – not that I don't believe you," he said quickly as I opened my mouth. "The police haven't exactly embraced using magic as part of their investigations, and mundane detective work doesn't cut it when we're working against spell craft. Tell me what you know and how I can be of assistance."

"Due to the results from our beads and our preliminary interviews, we have reason to believe that the fire was deliberately lit by a third party to gain access to the sanctuary."

Altan opened the pouch on his belt. Out of the corner of my eye, I noticed Barracks tense a little. Holding up a green bead, Altan said, "Don't worry, this one is harmless: it's a healing bead. You would have seen these before, yes?"

Barracks eyed the pouch curiously. "Yes, we do have access to healing beads, though a lot of the older officers refuse to use them."

"Why?" I asked.

"Prejudice?" Altan suggested before Barracks could respond.

The officer looked a little flustered. "Not prejudice exactly. They just don't trust what they don't know, so they don't use them unless they are specifically instructed to do so."

"Do you?"

"Use beads? Sure, sometimes. But some of them don't seem to do much. We haven't exactly been trained in their use."

"Wait a sec." Altan held up a hand. "Do you mean to say that sometimes you chuck a bead at the ground without knowing what it can do?"

Barracks had the grace to look embarrassed. "'Fraid so."

"For fuck's sake!" Altan growled low in his throat. "Are you kidding me?"

"Are you offering to train us?" Barracks countered.

"I don't have time," the sphinx snarled, his tail twitching.

"But if you trained us, we'd all have more time because you wouldn't be re-doing our work for us."

Altan stared at Barracks pensively for a long moment. "You make a good point." He scrubbed a hand over his face. "Here's a quick example to show you how useful the beads can be." He pulled out another one; this one was small with yellow spots.

He threw it against the floor and waited. The yellow spots grew brighter and left the bead, spiralling away from where we were sitting and drawing hundreds of golden lines on the blue carpet. The lines flared white before disappearing and leaving odd powdery tracks of residue all over the floor. "This bead leaves this residue on any biological evidence: strands of hair, faecal matter, skin flakes, you name it."

Barracks sat forward in his chair and gazed at the floor in wonder. "That is amazing!"

Altan dusted his hands. "Training in bead use is a problem for the future... right now, we need to focus on the fire at the sanctuary. From using a bead there, we've learnt that a spell was cast at the point of entry." At the look on Barracks' face, he elaborated. "The boundary ward was magically broken, which wouldn't have been possible with a standard bushfire. We suspect the person who broke in may have stolen something."

Barracks dropped his head in his hands. "That's not good. There's a push at the moment to close cases, and I'm afraid I've been too caught up in it." He bit his lip and flicked his eyes to the corner of the room where a security camera was watching us.

He lowered his voice. "Right now my hands are tied, but keep working that angle. I'll see what I can do to reopen the case and get the arson squad to give you some resources."

Altan nodded. "I appreciate that. How can we contact you directly?"

"Here." Barracks held out a card with his name, rank, police identification number and contact details on it. "I'll do everything I can to help but unfortunately, when it comes to magic-related crime, sometimes that's not much."

We'd left the police station and were now eating chicken wraps in the car overlooking green parklands. "Don't you think it's odd that no one wants to talk about Reginald Chatsworth?" I asked around a mouthful of food.

"Yes and no," Altan replied. "He's the sanctuary's patron, and I suppose they want to keep him happy by protecting him so he doesn't withdraw his support. However, we do need to talk to him. Why don't you call him now?"

I gulped down my food. "*Me*? What do I say?" Nervousness fluttered in my gut. Why did I suddenly feel so anxious about making a call? Was it because the person of interest had a title?

"If I wasn't here, what would you say?"

I took a deep breath and thought about it. "I'd ask him about his relationship with the sanctuary: how long he's been involved with it and what he provides. I'd ask where he was at the time of the fire and if anyone can confirm it." I shrugged. "And then I guess I'd just go from there, based on his answers."

"That's as good as anything I would do." Altan smiled and held out his phone.

I tried calling Lord Chatsworth, but it went straight to voicemail. I frowned and left a message then passed Altan's phone back to him and took another mouthful of my chicken wrap.

When the phone pinged, I shot him a hopeful look. "Nope. Not Chatsworth." He sighed. "But I do need to make a few calls for some other claims I'm working on, so I'm going to step out of the car for ten minutes. I want you to review the sanctuary's insurance policy schedule, as well as their Product Disclosure Statement. Check there are no limitations or exclusions on their cover, okay?"

I nodded mutely, my mouth still full. Once he'd closed the door, I groaned loudly. This was my least favourite part of the job. I'd had to do it in my old job, too, and it still sucked. Opening my tablet, I opened the attachments tab of the claim, selected the policy wording and started reading.

Chapter Eleven

When Altan returned to the car, I confirmed there were no relevant exclusions unless we found the fire to be arson by the owner. "I thought not, but it's always best to check," he replied slowly, gazing into the distance.

"Are you okay?" I asked. "You're off in a world of your own."

He gave himself a shake. "I'm fine, but I do need to take care of some other work. Can I drop you home?"

"Do you need my help?"

"Not with this, but thanks for the offer. Don't worry, your workload will increase in time." He gave a crooked smile and my heart fluttered in response. It really was the most disobedient organ. How many times would my head have to tell it to calm down before it finally listened?

As soon as Altan had dropped me home, I changed my clothes, grabbed my reusable grocery bags and headed to the shops. Millie would kill me if I didn't pick up food today.

In the supermarket, it made a change not to have to add up the cost of my groceries as I chose them. Out of habit I still kept a rough tally, but with my wages from my job I had no need to budget so strictly. Of course, I still paid attention to specials and I didn't spend frivolously, but it was so nice not to be riddled with anxiety every time I had to pay for something.

Once I'd gone through the checkout line and left the shop, I headed back to my car. A thrill of pleasure ran through me as I admired my beautiful tyres. I'd finally had enough money to replace them all, plus I'd been able to update the wards around my car and home. I sighed happily. They said money couldn't buy happiness – but it sure helped with your stress levels.

Chucking the groceries into my boot, I hopped into my sedan and immediately cranked up the air-conditioning. If this was the temperature in September, I was dreading the arrival of summer. I'd just checked my rearview and side mirrors and shifted the gear-stick to reverse when a familiar flash of blue hair near the trolley return made me pause. Was that Destiny?

I took my car out of gear and craned my neck to get a better look. She was talking to someone, although 'talking' was too passive of a word for the gestures she was making and the volume of her voice. I couldn't make out her words, so I cracked open my window to hear what she was saying.

"I'll pay you well, Anna. C'mon! You gotta help a girl out!"

Anna? Did she mean the vet? I adjusted my seat slowly so as not to draw attention to myself and shifted to get a better look. Destiny moved slightly and I finally saw the vet holding some green reusable shopping bags. "I can't help you, Destiny," I heard her say.

"It's only a little bit of blood – it won't be missed. I need it!"

"You don't need it, you *want* it."

"Anna, I'm seriously fucked if you don't help me. The loan shark has been sniffing around and I'm skint. I asked Todd for an advance, but you know that he can't help." Destiny pulled anxiously at her blue ponytail.

"Get a second job, then," Anna advised unsympathetically.

"I already have a second job! It's not enough," Destiny wailed.

"How can you pay me for unicorn blood if you can't even pay the guy who's going to physically harm you if you don't give him his money?" Anna's voice remained measured even in the face of Destiny's tears.

"I know a guy who can sell it on the black market for me. It depends on how much blood I can get, but it's worth a thousand dollars an ounce. I'd be able to pay the shark and you, and still have some money left over. There's no risk to you, I swear. I'll never tell anyone where I got it from."

"I don't do that," Anna said and wrinkled her nose.

"I know it's bad, but—"

"I'm sorry you're in trouble, Destiny, but you made your bed and now it's time for you to lie in it. I would *never* sell a magica's parts on the black market. Who knows what they'd be used for? The trade is illegal for a reason."

"Don't you fucking judge me," Destiny snarled. "You don't know what it's like!"

"I can't help you," Anna repeated bluntly. "Move aside."

"You've got to." Destiny was pleading now. "I'll do anything."

The car was heating up and a drop of sweat dripped down my temple. I slowly reached forward to move the air-conditioning onto my face, doing my best not to draw attention. As the dusty air from the vent hit me, I sneezed violently. Anna looked up and saw me. Turning back to the young woman, she said, "Destiny, you have an audience. I suggest you get out of here and don't ask me again."

Destiny spotted me and froze, her eyes wide. So much for remaining undetected. Then she took off, racing to her car and throwing herself in before peeling out of the carpark.

Well, that didn't look dodgy at all!

Anna sighed and shook her head. She gave me an awkward wave then carried her groceries over to her van.

I called Altan. Not wasting time on pleasantries, I said, "Something weird just happened."

"Are you okay?" His voice was immediately filled with concern.

"I'm fine. I was at the supermarket buying groceries and when I went to leave, I saw Destiny and Anna arguing in the carpark." I relayed as much of the conversation as I could remember.

"Well done, Trix. That's twice now that Destiny has appeared untrustworthy. We'll need to pin her down and have a more extensive interview tomorrow."

"Sure thing. How're the other claims going?"

A woman spoke to him in the background, and he murmured a reply. My gut twisted. Did he have a wife? I'd never asked him outright. All these feelings that I was fighting might need to be properly squashed if he was already taken.

Altan's voice came down the line. "I'm just helping Ros out, but we'll be done soon. After that I'm heading home to write up some reports."

I noticed he had said 'I' and not 'we', so maybe there wasn't anyone in his life. "Do you have a wife?" I blurted out, then clapped a hand over my mouth, mortified.

I couldn't believe I'd just asked that out loud. Oh well, I supposed it was one way to find out his relationship status.

He burst out laughing. Once his chuckles had subsided, he said, "No, Trix. I don't. Thanks for checking. Why, did you have someone in mind?" His coy tone did strange things to my insides.

"Nope, definitely not," I replied firmly. "Anyway, I'll let you get back to it. See you tomorrow. Bye, Altan."

"I'll talk to you soon," he said softly. "Bye, Trix."

My silly heart was doing that thing again where it refused to listen to my head. Oh, boy; I was going to get myself into trouble.

Chapter Twelve

A PECULIAR SMELL ASSAULTED my nose when I opened my front door, my arms loaded with shopping bags. I sniffed, looked around for the culprit – and froze.

I stared at my living room. I knew this was my house: that was my house number on the street, and I'd just walked through my front door. But the inside of my house looked all wrong.

"What. Did. You. Do?" I demanded, my voice shrill as I dropped the shopping bags with a thump.

What kind of psychopath moved around another person's furniture without asking first?

My mother sauntered down the hallway and fluttered her hands in the direction of the room. "I'm just trying to help. The energy in your house is all messed up. I learnt the art of feng shui in Hong Kong last year. Your home needed to be saged too, but I didn't know where to get sage from around here, so I grabbed some branches from the tree in the backyard and used that to smudge the room. It will help with the bad vibes."

There was only one bad vibe in this house, and it had nothing to do with the way the furniture was arranged. Gritting my teeth, I hissed, "Next time, don't bother helping."

Ignoring the hurt on my mother's face, I stalked to my bedroom, grabbed my stick and stomped outside. Sure, feng shui and saging had their place, but not in my home without my consent.

I walked straight up to my tea tree and found the broken branches. As I stood in front of it, its scent curled around me. Not the foul smell of burning that lingered in my house but the zesty bite of eucalyptus and mint. Reaching out to the tree, I shuddered when a wave of pain rolled through me. The torn remains of where the branches had been looked like deep wounds, and the tree's sap was pooling over the gashes.

Tears pricked my eyes as the tree wept in front of me. It was hurt.

"I'm sorry," I whispered and leant my head against its greyish bark. "You're in pain." I stroked the tree trunk, not caring that I looked insane, then I closed my eyes and took some deep breaths.

My feet were bare, and warmth from both my stick and the earth beneath my toes surged through me. I allowed the peculiar sense of strength and heat to gather inside me before I pushed it towards the damaged tea tree.

After a few seconds, the warmth faded, and fatigue overtook me. I sagged against the tree while my ears rang. Shaking my head to try and clear the noise, I looked at the trunk in front of me. Small buds of greenery were already covering the wounds, and the sap had congealed.

I stared. Had I done that?

"Good job," came a voice in my head.

I started, before realising it was Froggy. "Why am I not surprised that you're not surprised that apparently I can heal trees now?"

Froggy lifted her wings in her version of a shrug.

"Can't tell me, I guess?"

"The Everlasting Oath forbids me. But like I've told you before, you can figure it out on your own. I know it."

I studied her. "I'll keep trying. I just wish you could give me some clues."

The tawny frogmouth cocked her head, widening her yellow eyes as she did. *"You will receive an invitation soon. It would be best if you accepted it. It may help you find the answers you seek."*

"Ah. Another of your premonitions, I take it?"

Froggy nodded before looking at something over my shoulder. Her tail bobbed and her head drooped while her eyes grew pensive. She raised her beak to the sky and froze so that she looked exactly like a tree branch and blended into her surroundings.

I straightened and turned around to find my mother standing at the back door, watching me. "Come inside, Trix. It's too hot. Your hair is already so frizzy," she said.

"Gee, thanks, Mum," I muttered under my breath while battling the urge to pat my hair flat.

She opened her mouth to say something else but stopped when we were interrupted by Nic's yell from inside. Puzzled, I managed to take three steps before my friend raced out, holding my phone. "It's ringing!" she said and threw it at me.

I fumbled the catch but managed not to drop it. The screen showed that it was my friend Ellie calling. She didn't often phone me, she usually just texted. I hoped the elf was okay.

"Hey, Ellie, you all right?"

"Trix! How's tricks?" The male voice was not the one I was expecting. Ellie's brother, Perry, must have borrowed her phone.

"Oh hey, Perry. It's been an interesting day, to say the least. How're you? Is everything okay with Ellie and Isabella?"

"Yes, everything is perfect, and even more so now that I've heard your beautiful voice."

I shifted uncomfortably. "Oh, um, thanks." I should probably give him a compliment back, but I couldn't think of anything to say.

"I won't beat around the bush, Trix. Ellie mentioned you were home after your work trip away and I wanted to ask if I could take you to dinner."

"Dinner?" I exclaimed. "As in, like a date?"

Nicole grinned and started dancing on the spot and waving her arms around wildly. My mother pursed her lips and folded her arms.

"Yes, as in a date." Perry chuckled. "Are you free tonight?"

"Tonight?" I squeaked.

Nicole glared at me and gave an exaggerated nod of her head. "Yes, you are," she mouthed.

"I'm not sure," I hedged. "I've got a few jobs to do..."

Nic snatched the phone out of my hands and said, "Hey, Perry! I'm Nicole, Trix's best friend. Yes, she's free tonight. What time will you be here? In an hour? Perfect. I'll make sure she's ready." Then she hung up.

"What the heckin' heck, Nic!" I wanted to dance with rage. I didn't want to go on a date with Perry.

But then Altan's face floated into my mind's eye, and I stopped. I'd been obsessing for far too long over my boss. Maybe it would be a good idea to distract myself with someone more appropriate. It wasn't like I was committing to marry Perry if I went on one date. And he was a very nice guy, not to mention he was easy on the eye.

"Ugh. Fine. I'll go have a quick shower and get dressed."

"Do you really think that's a good idea, Trix?" my mother demanded. "Letting Millie see you going out on a date with a strange man, and on a school night, no less? What kind of example are you setting?"

"A better one than you did," sniped Nic. "Come on, Trix, let's go."

She draped an arm over my shoulders and led me away from Val. "I'll pack away the groceries while you get changed, and then I'll keep an eye on Millie tonight. You go out and have some fun for a change. Don't let the old bat get you down – you're allowed to have fun. Don't forget to wear a dress and heels, okay? I don't care how much they hurt your feet."

I cleaned myself up in record time. As I put on my little black dress, I recalled the last time I had worn it back in Bowen when I was pretending to hit on that poor sap at the bar. That had been followed by the battle with the komada. How on earth the dress hadn't been shredded from the ensuing dash through the bush, I'd never know. It had taken a few washes and some hand scrubbing, but thankfully, the saliva from the komada's mouth had eventually washed out.

A quick brush of make-up in the form of eye liner, mascara and lipstick, and I was ready. Nic appeared behind me holding strappy black stilettos. "No," I protested. "No way in the seven kingdoms of the Hellscape are you getting me to wear those."

My friend gave an evil cackle. "If you don't wear them, I'm going to burn your entire wardrobe to ash and go on a shopping spree for you. I promise you won't like what I buy."

I stared at her in horror. "You would never."

She pulled a box of matches from her pocket. "Wouldn't I?" Her wide smile that showed too many teeth made her look slightly unhinged.

Narrowing my eyes, I snatched the ankle breakers from her. "I wear these under duress. Just leave my clothes alone."

Chapter Thirteen

When there was a knock at my door, I suddenly felt the urge to pee again even though it would be the fourth time since I'd arrived home from work. I told myself it was just nerves and ignored my bladder.

Nic, Millie and my mother were sitting in the lounge room watching a movie, but at the sound of the knock they all poked their heads over the back of the couch. Nicole pumped her eyebrows suggestively, Millie gave an awkward thumbs up, while my mother looked disgruntled.

Smoothing the front of my dress, I fixed a smile on my face and hoped my hands wouldn't shake too much.

I opened the door. "Hi." My welcoming smile froze as I tried to take in what I was seeing.

Pink clouded my vision, and I wondered if I was hallucinating. When my brain finally made sense of what my eyes were telling it, I realised a giant bunch of pink roses was filling the door frame. They shifted and Perry poked his head out to one side of them.

"Good evening, Beatrix." Somehow, he managed to bow while still holding the roses. "You look ravishing tonight."

My mouth opened and closed like a fish starved of oxygen before I snapped it shut, and my manners kicked in. Wobbling on my heels, I bobbed an awkward curtsy. "Thank you, sir."

"Please accept this humble gift in exchange for the pleasure of your company."

"Wow. They're...they're something else, aren't they? Shall I just pop them in a vase?" I didn't know what the protocol was with gift giving and I had no idea if I had a vase big enough to hold the gigantic bunch... but I couldn't just leave them laying on the table.

"They already have their own vase. Where is your sitting room? Or I could put them on your hall table? I'll take care of the flowers. No need to risk dirtying your beautiful dress."

"I don't have a sitting room or a hall table," I said slowly. The difference in our social standing was already obvious and technically the date hadn't even started yet.

"Silly me," he said smoothly. "I forget how formal some elven families can be. That's fine. You just show me where you'd like them, and I'll set them down for you."

I hadn't had a chance to do the dishes, and I knew I'd feel mortified if he saw the kitchen the way it was. As soon as I had that thought, I gave myself a stern talking to. If he liked me, he had to accept me the way I was, regardless of whether I was any good at washing dishes.

"This way," I said, my voice a little higher pitched than I'd intended. The nerves were really doing a number on me today. I certainly didn't find Perry comfortable to be around, not the way Altan was. I shoved the sphinx out of my mind; this was not the time to be thinking about another man.

Once he'd placed the roses down on my dining table, I got a good look at him. He was wearing a beautifully tailored suit, obviously made to measure. Oh, frick-a-fracking frog's legs. How fancy was this restaurant going to be?

"Now, before I forget, Ellie asked me to pass this on to you. She apologises she can't give it to you in person but she's heading to the airport tonight and won't be home until later in the week." He pulled a stiff vellum envelope from his jacket and handed it to me with a flourish. "An invitation for the lady." He bowed again.

I blinked. "When she said I'd get an invitation soon, she wasn't kidding," I murmured, thinking of Froggy's premonition.

"What was that?" Perry asked, a look of confusion crossing his features.

"Huh? Oh, nothing. Thank you." I slid a finger under the edge of the envelope and broke the wax seal. It was the most formal-looking invitation I had ever received: thick, embossed parchment inscribed with fancy calligraphy. I quickly scanned it; it was inviting me to a charity gala on Friday evening in support of the Magica Sanctuary of Queensland.

Froggy was right. This would be the perfect opportunity to discover who had started the fire... if we hadn't already figured out the culprit by then.

Perry interrupted my thoughts by saluting the three women on the couch then offered me his arm with a charming smile. I accepted nervously, hoping desperately that he wouldn't touch my hands because they were slick with sweat.

With a sigh I reminded myself that I had to give the guy a chance. Just because things felt easy with Altan didn't mean they couldn't be easy with Perry, too. I just needed to relax and try to enjoy the night.

As he led me out the front door, I waved a hurried farewell to my loved ones then jolted to a stop when I saw the red convertible sitting in my driveway. My jaw dropped. "Blimey!" I squeaked after a moment. "Nice car."

"She's my baby." He grinned happily. "It's the one indulgence I allow myself outside of the kitchen." He released me, opened the passenger door and bowed for a third time. "Your chariot awaits, my lady."

I teetered on my heels as I got into the car; I certainly didn't feel like a lady. "Thank you," I murmured as he gently shut the door.

Staring at the interior, I tried not to move because I was terrified I'd break something. I clasped my hands together and tried to stop my heels from marking the floor mat.

"So where are we going?" I asked, hoping that some conversation would help me relax and stop thinking about sweating on the fancy leather seat.

"One of my restaurants," he replied.

I frowned. "Wait... are you cooking?"

"No, no. I own and manage four different restaurants, but I only cook occasionally in one of them."

"Wow. That must keep you busy."

"It certainly does," he replied smoothly. "But not too busy to spend an evening with a ravishing woman like you."

I flushed then chuckled nervously. "Thank you for the compliment," I replied. The words felt stiff and strange, and I tried to push the awkward feeling away. I had to relax if this was going to work. "It's really impressive that you manage four restaurants. Tell me more about what that looks like."

Perry launched into a description of his average week and some of the stories of wrong orders, missing ingredients and emotional outbursts from the staff had me laughing. By the end of the drive, I'd almost forgotten my discomfort.

He pulled up in front of a swanky-looking restaurant, hopped out and rushed around to my door to open it for me. Passing his keys to a valet, he took my arm and led me through the revolving door. I was grateful to lean on him as I wobbled my way inside; walking in heels wasn't getting any easier.

The maître d' greeted Perry formally and offered me a friendly smile before leading us to a secluded table partially shielded by large ferns at the back of the restaurant.

The place dripped with elegance and expense. A crystal chandelier hung in the centre of the room, while plush red seats and heavy, champagne-coloured tablecloths added to the opulence. Classic artwork in golden frames decorated the walls and large glazed pots filled with greenery dotted the floor, offering each guest their own secluded oasis. I could only see ten tables in the whole restaurant.

Perry pulled out a chair for me and I sat down obediently, then glanced at the menu on the table. I gulped when I saw the prices. Bile coiled in my stomach and threatened to fill my mouth. I knew the place was fancy, but it obviously catered to the upper class.

Perry must have noticed my expression because he flashed a boyish grin. "Don't worry, I've got this." When I began to protest that it was too much, he cut me off. "Don't stress. The owner doesn't have to pay." He winked at me.

The waiter came over, asked for our drinks order and Perry ordered two glasses of white wine. When he saw my expression he said, "It pairs beautifully with the first course."

"I don't usually drink much white wine. It gives me a terrible headache."

He waved his hand dismissively and corrected me. "*Cheap* white wine gives you a headache. This is the good stuff. You'll be fine."

He continued talking about the restaurant. While his stories were interesting, there was a sour taste in my mouth because he hadn't allowed me to choose my own food or drink. And neither had he bothered to ask me anything about myself.

As the night went on, I had to give him credit: the white wine did pair beautifully with the scallops and lemon foam. Even so, that didn't change my feeling that we weren't compatible. I listened politely and laughed in the right places, but I started yawning at eight o'clock in an effort to wrap the night up early.

After eating seven delicious but tiny courses, Perry drove me home. A text pinged on my phone during the drive, and I glanced at it. It was Altan saying how impressed he was by my work again. A warm glow filled my chest, and a smile tugged at my lips.

It felt wrong to respond to his message while I was in the car with Perry, so I returned the phone to my clutch and tried to focus on my date's conversation. Once we'd pulled onto the driveway, I got out quickly to avoid any awkward lingering in an enclosed space. "Thanks so much for a lovely evening," I said, walking to my door as fast as I could on the high heels. He caught up to me and offered his arm again. I took it reluctantly, but only so I wouldn't break an ankle.

"You're so welcome. I had a wonderful night." The elf paused then added, "I hope you did, too."

"The food at your restaurant is amazing," I said truthfully. "It's not somewhere I could ever afford so I'm really grateful for the opportunity to sample it."

"We can go anytime."

"That's very kind of you to offer, thank you." I fished my keys out of my bag, hoping he'd got the hint.

He leant forward and gave me a peck on the cheek. It was such a shame. He was attractive, successful and sweet, but I couldn't get over the feeling that we'd never be equal if we were in a relationship. "Good night," I murmured and gave him a final wave before dashing through my front door and shutting it in his face.

Thank the wolf's moon that was over. I was exhausted.

But the night's ordeal wasn't *quite* finished. Millie and Val were nowhere to be seen but Nic's head popped over the back of the couch again. She frowned, then bounced into the kitchen where I was dumping my clutch on the counter so I could lean against the bench while I de-heeled myself.

She stood in front of me, legs akimbo and hands on hips, staring at me reproachfully. "You're home early. What happened?"

I decided to lay it all out for her. "He's a lovely man and very wealthy, but he's not right for me."

Nic raised her eyes to the heavens. "That's what you always say!"

"It is not! I've never dated someone with that much money."

She sighed dramatically. "That's not what I mean. You always have an issue with the men you date."

I handed back the heels. "Look, Nic, I appreciate your concern. I know it's because you care about me. And I also know that you worry that I'm not dating for Millie's sake, or because I'm not over Chris, but it's not that. The thing is, I'd rather be alone for the rest of my life than with the wrong man."

Nicole eyed me suspiciously as if trying to determine if I was telling the truth. Apparently satisfied with what she saw on my face, she said, "Fine. Just promise me that you'll keep your eyes peeled and your mind open, okay? The right man might be hiding in plain sight."

Her words reminded me that I was overdue in texting Altan back.

Was I going to analyse the correlation between Nic's comment and where my brain went?

Absolutely not.

"Mu-uum!" My daughter's cry echoed through the house, rousing me from my slumber. It was as familiar now as it had been when it was the only thing she'd said as a toddler. At least now she could feed herself. "Have you been shopping yet?" she yelled.

"Have you used your eyes and actually looked?" I shouted back as I dragged myself out of bed and into the kitchen.

"Yeah, but there's nothing to eat." Her head was buried in the pantry.

"Nothing to eat? I think you'll find there's plenty. I went shopping yesterday."

She spoke over me. "Can I get tuckshop again?"

"Surely you can find something that tickles your fancy?" I joined her at the pantry. "Just because we have a little more money now doesn't mean we can start spending frivolously. Unless there really is no food, I'd rather you only bought lunch from school once a week, okay?"

"But other kids get it *more* than once per week," she whined.

I raised my eyebrows at the pushback. What was happening to my sweet girl who accepted everything without complaint? I sighed. I'd known it couldn't last forever, but — perhaps naively — I'd hoped that I'd gotten away without having to deal with any teen attitude or hormones.

"I'm sure not every other kid gets tuckshop multiple days per week," I responded. "And even if they do, these are the rules in this family. Those kids are not part of this family, unlucky for them."

"Fine, just thought I'd check." Millie shrugged, her brief rebellion over before it had really begun. "I'll make a jam sandwich."

I quirked an eyebrow, feeling like I might get whiplash if her changes in attitude got any worse.

I left her putting together the food for her lunchbox and started getting ready for work. During our chat, my mother had risen, hair wild, eyes bleary, and stumbled out to pour herself a coffee.

"Good morning, Mum," I greeted her as I rinsed my mug.

She studied me over the lip of her coffee mug. "If you've got so much money from your new job, why don't you let Millie get tuckshop more than once a week?"

"Please stop trying to undermine me in front of my daughter," I said bluntly. It was too early in the morning to deal with my mother's passive aggressive behaviour.

Her eyes flew wide in what I'm sure she thought was a look of innocence. "I'm not! It's an honest question. You mentioned you're on good money now, but Millie doesn't seem to be benefiting from it."

Instantly seething, I slammed my hand flat on the countertop. "How dare you?"

Millie froze, still holding her lunchbox and water bottle, and stared at us. Nic raced into the kitchen and snatched her arm. "I'll take Millie to the bus stop," she yelled. "See you tonight!" As Nic dragged my daughter out of the kitchen, she grabbed her school bag and sneakers, shoved Millie out the front door ahead of her, then slammed it behind them.

My mother and I glared at each other. "You are crossing so many lines." I kept my voice pitched low in an effort to keep my anger in check.

"I'm just telling you what I'm seeing. I would hate for Millie to miss out because you're so focussed on your new job and going on dates that you forget you're a mother."

The rage that filled me made my chest tight and tears prick at my eyes. I pointed a quivering finger at her. "You don't get to make comments on my skills as a mother! You are not qualified! I will not sit here and listen to your insults when you don't know what I've done – and continue to do – for Millie. I know that I'm doing my best. I know that I'm enforcing healthy boundaries and rules, and I know that I'm doing more than you ever did for me."

"Trix!" she cried. "How could you say that?"

I held up a hand to silence her. "I have to go to work. I don't want to continue this conversation right now because if I do, I know I'll say something that I'll regret."

Snatching up my bag and work tablet, I stalked away from her and stomped out to the kerb. My breath was coming in short, laboured pants as if I'd just run a marathon. Even seeing Altan's car appear around the corner a few minutes later did nothing to calm my fury.

As I flung myself into the car, the sphinx raised an elegant eyebrow and studied me. "Do you want to talk about it?"

"Nope. Distract me, please."

He pulled away from the kerb and started talking. "Certainly. I actually have a question for you. I've been invited to a charity ball on Friday evening in support of the sanctuary. I thought maybe you'd like to come with me as my guest. For the claim, of course. We might learn something valuable."

"Oh." Taken aback, I groped for a reply. "Thank you for asking me, but I'm already going. I received a formal invitation from Perry... well, it was from Ellie, but Perry gave it to me."

"Perry?" Altan's ears flicked. "You mean Periadonus, Ellie's brother?" I nodded. "When were you talking to him?"

"Last night. He...he took me to dinner."

Was it my imagination, or did Altan's hands just tighten on the steering wheel?

"As in, like a date?" His voice was flat.

"I suppose *he* thought it was one. When he called to ask me out, Nic stole my phone and told him I'd go out with him. He's a lovely elf, but he and I aren't a match." I glanced at the sphinx.

He released a breath, and his shoulders relaxed. "Sorry to hear that." A small smile played on his lips.

"You don't look sorry," I muttered under my breath.

"What was that?" he asked.

"Nothing," I responded quickly.

He sniggered. "Anyway... Before we start the day, why don't we discuss the case over a coffee from Bards and Beans?"

"That's the best thing you could ever have suggested to me this morning." I fist-pumped the air.

He loosed a short bark of laughter. "I'm happy to know that I please you."

A shiver of delight coursed through me at his choice of words, but I shook it off; they didn't mean anything special.

Altan wove expertly through the local traffic and somehow managed to find a parking space right outside the popular café within twenty minutes of leaving my house.

Picking up my bag and work tablet, I stepped out of the car and somehow managed to trip *up* the kerb. With my hands full, I had no way to save myself from faceplanting. As the pavement rushed towards me, I didn't even have time to choke out a yelp – but then my fall was halted. Altan's arms and tail wrapped around my torso and saved me in the nick of time.

Pulling me upright, he carefully patted my armour, tucking and adjusting to ensure it was still sitting correctly. "Are you alright?" he asked. The warmth in his voice and the concern in his eyes filled me with the same delight I'd felt in the car.

Clearing my throat, I replied, "Yes, I'm fine. Thanks to you."

"It was nothing," he murmured. His tail was still wrapped around my waist, which he seemed to realise at the same time I did. Stepping back, he ran his fingers through his dark hair.

I felt the loss of his closeness keenly. Giving myself an internal shake, I hoisted my bag's strap over my shoulder and glanced at the tablet to make sure it was undamaged. I had to get a grip on myself. Seriously, I couldn't keep feeling like a mopey teenager every time he wasn't touching me. This was getting ridiculous.

An awkward silence stretched between us as we entered the café.

The drone of voices chatting provided a constant background noise. Fairies flitted around, dodging the hanging plants while they took orders and delivered food and drink. The plates were almost as big as they were; it was a miracle that they didn't break more dishes.

The coffee grinder was working constantly behind the counter to keep up with the morning rush. The miniature wyverns were sitting on a bed of coals, only venturing out of their enclosure to froth and warm the milk with their breath. The fairies claimed that was the secret to their wildly popular coffee.

Altan led me to a booth overlooking a water fountain in Bards and Beans' internal courtyard. It was surrounded by an explosion of colourful flowers, and butterflies flitted constantly in and out of the blooms. I sighed with contentment and rested my chin on my hands. "It's so beautiful here. I don't get here very often. But their coffee is amazing every time." I glanced at him. "Thank you for suggesting it."

Altan's face lit up with pleasure. "I'm glad you like it."

I melted. Then threw a metaphorical bucket of cold water over myself. I really needed to cool down. We were here for work.

I placed the tablet on the table and opened the claim file while Altan turned to the fairy that had just arrived and ordered our coffees. Then I froze: he'd remembered how I liked my coffee.

After the fairy had flown away to the kitchen, he caught me staring at him and looked stricken. "I'm sorry, I should have checked. Did you want that sort of coffee today? I can call them back and get you what you want?"

He started to raise his hand to attract the waiter's attention, but I grabbed it. "No, it's perfect. I just didn't realise you'd paid attention to my order in the past. I don't even remember ordering coffee in front of you. That's really sweet. Thank you."

His fingers curled around mine and my heart stuttered in my chest. Here I was trying to remain professional, and then he went and held my hand. He really wasn't playing fair.

"Trix..." Altan started but then hesitated and looked down at our entwined hands on the tabletop.

"Beatrix!" A woman's voice hailed me from across the café, attracting our attention, not to mention that of the customers at the nearby tables.

I pulled back, feeling like I'd been caught with my hand in the cookie jar. He slowly withdrew his own hand and scanned the room. The woman who'd yelled out to me was coming over to our table, her grey hair bouncing merrily as she ducked around the other customers.

I blinked. "Mrs Hinschen! This is a pleasant surprise!"

"Oh, Beatrix! I keep telling you to call me Jane!" she exclaimed.

I chuckled. "And I keep telling you to call me Trix."

She smacked her forehead lightly with the palm of her hand. "You do, too! Sorry, Trix! One of these days I'll remember."

As an aside to Altan, I explained, "Mrs Hinschen was an old client of mine from when I worked at Maroochydore Mundane and Magica Insurance Brokers."

Jane glanced at Altan and flashed me a mischievous smile. "And are you going to introduce me to your boyfriend now?"

Colour rushed to my cheeks; I wished I *could* call him that. Altan was watching but he said nothing. Why wasn't he correcting her? And was he *smiling*?

"No, no! Altan isn't my boyfriend." I stumbled on the word. "He's training me in my new job – he's basically my supervisor."

Jane folded her arms in mock disappointment. "Best-looking supervisor I've ever met. I wish they'd had bosses like you in my working days." She fluttered her eyelashes before giving a jolly guffaw. "No disrespect to my dear Howard, of course, not that he's around anymore. He was a wonderful man, but he wasn't much of a looker. But that's okay because I was pretty enough for both of us back then."

"You're still pretty now, madam." Altan grinned at her.

"Oh, what a charmer he is!" Jane's hands fluttered over her chest. "I'm not much good at playing Cupid, but I think that you two should go on a date."

My cheeks felt flaming hot. "But that would be...unprofessional."

"Unprofessional, schmunprofessional. Personally, I feel like you're overthinking this."

I sighed and muttered, "I'm good at doing that." I met Altan's gaze; instead of looking embarrassed or annoyed by Jane's comments, his eyes were alight with curiosity. Uh-oh. What did that mean?

Thankfully, it was at that moment that our coffees arrived in their takeaway cups. I cleared my throat and took a sip of oat latte to cover my distress. "So how are you, Jane? What's been happening in the last couple of months?"

"SSDD," she replied solemnly.

I frowned: was that some sort of disease? "I'm sorry, what does that stand for?"

Altan chortled. The mischievous glint in Jane's eyes was back. "Oh my dear girl, you are naïve, aren't you? SSDD. Same shit, different day."

"Jane!" Somehow, I hadn't expected the sweet old lady to use profanities.

"What?" She looked at me innocently. Waving her hand, she changed the subject as fast as blow flies lay eggs on bin day. "I'm old and my life isn't nearly as interesting as yours. So tell me, how's the new job going? Or should I ask you later when your 'supervisor'," she used her fingers to make air quotes, "isn't listening?"

I chuckled. "No, it's fine. I love it. It's bloody hard but it's awesome. I've learnt so much and I'm getting stronger every week."

"Stronger?"

"Yeah. Altan is training me up so I can battle rogue magicas should the need arise. When we're out assessing a claim, we have to be ready to fight any magicas that try to stop our investigation."

"Oh my word, that sounds fascinating! What sort of training are you doing?"

"Initially, I needed to improve my fitness, but now I'm starting to work on my hand-to-hand combat, along with swordsmanship and archery. Altan is also teaching me how to use beads effectively against the different magicas."

Jane darted her hand towards my arm and squeezed my bicep. "Well now, that is fantastic." She looked at Altan admiringly. "Don't forget, if you ever need to work on your marksmanship, I know a lot about shotguns and rifles. I'd be happy to help."

"Thank you, Jane." I turned to Altan. "When I last renewed Jane's home and contents insurance, she told me she had an expensive Winchester that needed to be specified under her contents."

"Oh, I remember that day! The look on your face was priceless." She chuckled before telling the sphinx, "My late husband and I were heavily involved with the local gun club, and I still go out occasionally. It feels good to keep my eye in. I might be an old dog, but I'd love to teach Trix some of my tricks." She winked at me.

"All training is beneficial," Altan said warmly. "It's always a good idea to be a well-rounded warrior. Plus, other trainers can sometimes explain things in a different way that makes more sense to us. Why don't we pencil in a time for you to take Trix shooting?"

Jane clapped her hands. "Excellent! Let's make it happen." She gave me her number and promised she was free almost anytime, which was useful because my schedule was filling up fast.

I was about to ask how her daughter was when Altan's phone rang. He glanced at the screen before flipping it open. "Todd? What's wrong?" He listened for a few long seconds, his eyes narrowing. "Okay, we'll head straight there."

He stood abruptly. "Trix, we're needed at the sanctuary. Lovely to meet you, Jane. I'll make sure Trix books in a time with you to practise her target shooting." He bowed his head before offering me his hand.

"So formal." Jane sighed admiringly. "How lovely. Have a wonderful day, dear. I'll be waiting for your call!"

As we grabbed our takeaway cups off the table and hurried to the car, Altan filled me in. "There's been an incident at the sanctuary," he murmured in my ear.

His breath tickled my cheek and made me shiver. Pushing away my wayward thoughts, I focussed. "An incident? Is everyone okay?"

He waited to answer until we were both in the car and buckled up. "So far...but there's a griffin on the loose."

"Gosh darn griffins," I exclaimed with an exasperated groan. "Again? Seriously? Is it the one that we already fought?"

"Nope." His expression was grim as he released the handbrake. "Apparently, this was a wild griffin that broke *into* the sanctuary."

CHAPTER FIFTEEN

ABOUT FORTY MINUTES LATER we pulled into the sanctuary carpark, leapt out and ran past the office. All seemed quiet, but that wasn't necessarily a good thing. Swords drawn, Altan and I ran faster. Raised voices near the stable caught our attention and we rushed along the winding paths towards them.

When we rounded the last bend there wasn't a griffin in sight, but Destiny and Clyde were yelling at each other. Todd was in the middle, apparently trying to separate them.

"This was your fault, Clyde!" Destiny shouted. "That griffin would have never got inside the sanctuary if you'd done a half-decent job with the temporary fence. This wouldn't have happened if you didn't spend your days drinking and chasing griffins around trying to steal their feathers. Do us all a favour and go to therapy to sort out your shit!"

"Fuck off," slurred the gnome. His squeaky voice reduced the impact of his words. "You know, it wouldn't surprise me if you lit that fire yourself. Everyone knows that firies are pyromaniacs."

Destiny's hands curled into claws as she launched herself at him. "How dare you?" she screeched. "You absolute wanker! I'm going to kill you!"

"Hey!" Altan yelled. "What's going on here?" He ran forward and helped Todd pull them away from each other, then held Destiny's arms behind her while Todd wrapped his arms around Clyde and lifted the gnome off the ground.

"You can't do this!" shouted the gnome, windmilling his legs. "This is racist, or ableist, or specieist...or something! Put me down right now, asshole!" Todd lowered the gnome but kept a firm grip around his torso.

Destiny spat and glared daggers at Clyde. "It's his fault the griffin got inside the sanctuary. It attacked the enclosure with the other griffin in it, and now that'll need repairs by the druids. Expensive repairs."

"Where's the loose griffin now?" I asked.

"Flew away," grunted Todd as Clyde struggled against him. The gnome was surprisingly strong.

"Anyone hurt?"

Todd shook his head.

"Take him away," Altan instructed, nodding at the gnome. "Let's all just focus on calming down."

Once Todd and Clyde had disappeared in the direction of the office, Altan released Destiny. She stood sullenly, scuffing a shoe against the grass. "All right. We need some honest answers today, Destiny. What did Clyde mean about you being a pyromaniac?" he asked.

Destiny directed her scowl at him. "Don't you start. I am not a pyro. I used to volunteer with the rural fire brigade on my days off, that's all."

"You didn't think to mention that in our initial interview?"

"I didn't think it was relevant."

"There's been a fire in your place of work, and you didn't think it was relevant?" Altan's tone was incredulous.

She folded her arms. "I haven't been out to a fire with the crew in a few months. And it's not like I was called in to attend this one. I had nothing to do with it!"

"How do we know you're not lying?" Altan challenged her. I blinked, surprised at the bluntness of his question. Maybe I needed to work on not being so polite with suspects. "Where were you at the time of the fire?" he demanded.

"At home. Asleep," she growled.

"Can anyone corroborate your whereabouts?"

She bit her lip. "No. My boyfriend broke up with me last month. So no, I've got no one." Tears filled her eyes.

Oh, fairy dust. I wasn't equipped to handle this much emotion so early on a Wednesday morning. I looked at Altan in panic.

He softened and placed a hand on Destiny's shoulder. "I'm sorry to hear that. If you think of anyone that can give you an alibi or some way to prove you weren't anywhere near here at the time of the fire, let us know so we can remove you from our list. Okay?"

A nudge in my gut put me on high alert. I might have been overthinking again, but a part of me wondered if she was turning on the waterworks to gain our sympathy. I prodded, a little harshly, "Destiny, is there anything *else* you want to tell us?"

She looked at me before dropping her eyes; she knew what I was talking about. With a heavy sigh, she said, "Fine. I know you saw me yesterday. I shouldn't have asked Anna for the unicorn blood. And I shouldn't have run away."

She played nervously with a lock of her blue hair and spoke quickly, the story spilling out of her like a dam that had burst its banks. "Look, I owe money. My ex said he knew a good guy who could help me out, but it turned out he was a loan shark. I was late with a payment and now he's after me. My ex has jumped ship and I'm receiving threats. I'm scared." Her voice broke.

Ugh: now *I* felt like the bad guy. "I'm sorry," I said awkwardly. "Is there anything we can do to help?"

Destiny gave a bitter laugh. "Unless you have a spare twenty grand laying around, no, you can't. I should have vetted the guy and read the contract properly before agreeing to take out the loan. It's my own stupid fault."

I squeezed her arm. "Don't be like that. We all make mistakes. Can you get another job?"

"I've got two jobs already: I work here during the day, and I work nights as a waitress at a restaurant in Beerwah. That's why I've had to cut down volunteering with the rural fire brigade. I don't have enough hours in the day as it is."

"That's a tough situation to be in," I said sympathetically.

"What do *you* know?" she mumbled.

I held her gaze. "I'm a single mum working full-time, trying my best to give my daughter everything I never had. My situation *is* different to yours but trust me when I say I understand the stress of not having enough money."

Destiny sniffled then wiped her nose on the back of her sleeve. "Did you ever agree to borrow money from bad guys?"

"Well, no," I conceded. "That's something I can't help you with. But I have made a lot of mistakes, and in the moment it sucks. But eventually those bad moments become bad memories, and you find joy again." I patted her back reassuringly. "Now, why don't you tell us what happened this morning with the griffin?"

She rubbed her tear-stained face. "I was just finishing up my usual feeding routine when a young female griffin tore through the plastic fence and raced towards our injured griffin in the enclosure. She was only close to him for maybe a minute before Clyde came racing over twirling a lasso." She rolled her eyes. "As if that would catch a griffin. Anyway, he scared her, and she took off in a hurry. She dropped some feathers and, of course, he ran to pick them up." She screwed her nose up in disgust.

I didn't understand why she was so against him collecting griffin feathers. Was it a conservation issue? Or something else?

"I've been annoyed about Clyde's drinking for ages, and when he built that dodgy temporary fence, it really irked me," she went on. "But even after the griffin's break in, I just focussed on helping him fix the hole again. We're still waiting for the fencing contractor to do a permanent repair, but at least nothing should get in or out now. We were packing up when Clyde made some smartass comments about my newly single status, and I just lost it."

"Go have a drink of water and give Clyde some space for the rest of the day. And take some time out for yourself," Altan told her.

The maternal side of me insisted on giving Destiny a hug, and the young woman melted into my arms. With her head tucked under my chin, I stroked her blue hair, then ended the embrace with a gentle squeeze. "I know it feels impossible right now, but it will all work out in the end. I just know it will."

Chapter Sixteen

We left Destiny and walked back along the path towards the office. Before we'd even knocked, Todd threw open the door of the donga and urged us to come inside. "I've sent Clyde to sleep it off. Sorry you had to see that... but that's not why I called you over."

Altan and I shared a glance. "What is it?" I asked.

"I noticed something odd on the CCTV and I want a second opinion." He ran a hand over the five o'clock shadow on his chin. His eyes looked tired. "I don't know if it's something or nothing, but it's weird. The police have this footage too, and they haven't said anything to me, so maybe I'm just being paranoid."

Todd led us to his computer and pressed play. "This was from the night of the fire. Here we see the fire breach the boundary and break the wards – but look here." He paused the video and pointed at the screen. "Once the worst of the fire is over, there's a strange shadow that enters through the broken fence."

Altan leant forward to scrutinise the screen. "You're absolutely right. That's a human shadow. I'm sure of it. They must have some sort of invisibility spell cast over them. Are there any other camera angles?"

"Nothing more than what I've already sent you. We've only got security cameras at the carpark, here in the office, one on each boundary fence, in the feed room and in the potions' storeroom. I've been meaning to add more, but money is tight." He shrugged. "I'd rather spend the donations we receive on caring for the magicas."

"And Clyde set those cameras up for you?" I clarified.

Todd shifted uncomfortably. "Yes."

Thinking out loud, I asked, "So he knows where they are and how they work?"

"That's correct. Look, I don't want to suspect my employees of anything, but I need to do the right thing by the magicas. If Clyde has done something that could have harmed them, he's out." He winced and his voice was pained. "I doubt he'll get another job with his bad habits, but I have to put the sanctuary first."

Another thought popped into my head. "Clyde was the one who called you to report the fire, right?"

"Yeah. Initially I didn't believe him. He's called me in the past, drunk as a lorikeet who's been drinking fermented fruit, saying he can see all types of things."

I laid a hand on his arm. "Don't fire him yet, Todd. We're still investigating, and we don't have any proof that he's the arsonist."

Altan chimed in, "Did you send our office a copy of *all* the security footage you have?"

Todd nodded. "Yes. James, my husband, sent it to the first assessor. But I downloaded the clip I just showed you onto this as well, just in case." He handed me a USB stick.

"Perfect," Altan said. "We'll speak to one of our specialists about whether they can remove the invisibility spell from the video."

Todd's eyes widened. "You can do that?"

"It will depend on the spell, but sometimes we can. Leave it with us. Trix, let's go."

We walked quickly back to the car. As we climbed inside, I asked, "Sorry, Altan, I don't want to sound dumb, but can we really remove an invisibility spell from a video?"

"You don't need to apologise, Trix. You don't sound dumb. You don't know what you don't know. But that spell didn't remove their shadow from the footage so it's unlikely that it's of a particularly high quality. That tells me that we should be able to scrub it. I'll call Vic. You've met him, right? He's Ellie's husband."

I nodded. "I don't know him well, but I've met him. He showed me his bead-making workshop."

Altan shot me an envious look. "Lucky you! Vic's knowledge and skill with bead-making is unrivalled. He should be able to get us what we need."

As we drove back to the Sunshine Coast, he made the call through the car's Bluetooth speaker. "Hi, Vic. We've got a problem that needs a magical solution."

"Altan! Good to hear from you, my boy. Who is 'we'?"

"Trix and me."

"Ah, Ellie mentioned that young Trix had a new job at your company, though I didn't realise you were working together. That's wonderful. Hope you're taking care of the young lady?"

"I'm certainly trying my best... although some days she makes it difficult." He shot me a wry smile and mouthed 'komada'.

I huffed. At least I hadn't rushed headlong into danger during this claim. At least, not yet.

"Well, now," Vic went on. "I'm sure you're both doing a fine job. So tell me, what's this magical problem you have?"

"I need to know if you have a bead that can scrub a video of magical enhancements. We have security footage that appears to show a person covered by an invisibility spell and we need to reveal their identity."

Vic hesitated. "I don't have anything to hand that I can think of, though I'm sure I could make one for you. But I'll need time, and I'm booked out for the next month with a commission. You know I'll do what I can to fit you in, but this work is for the Inter-Magical Community Council, and they have to remain my priority at least for the next week. If you haven't found a work around in that time, give me another call and I'll see what I can do."

"No problem, Vic. Thanks anyway. We'll be in touch if we still need help." Altan hung up. Drumming his fingers against the steering wheel, he suddenly took the next exit.

"What are you doing?" I asked.

"I have another idea." Pulling into the side of the road, he flicked open his phone and clicked through his contact list.

"I'm surprised your dinosaur phone can connect to Bluetooth," I told him.

Ignoring me, he made another call. Caroline's perky voice answered after the first ring. "What can I do you for, Altan?"

"Your aunt. She's like you, yes?"

"You mean she's intelligent, hilarious and fabulous? Why yes, yes, she is."

"That's not what I meant."

Caroline huffed. "So how do you mean?"

"You mentioned that she was good at handling illusion magic. I need to know if she can scrub a video of magical enhancements. We have CCTV that appears to show a person covered by an invisibility spell."

"Oh, that's juicy! Yeah, Aunty Faith should be able to help you. She's working at the shop today until five o'clock."

"Hang on," I interrupted. "Did you say your aunt's name was Faith?"

"Yes, it is. Do you know her?" Caroline exclaimed.

I grinned. "I think so. I know a pixie called Faith who volunteers at my daughter's netball courts. She has pink hair."

"Oh, no way! That's her!"

"That's great and all," Altan interrupted. "But Caroline, can you please tell her to expect us within the hour?"

"Certainly can."

"Thanks." He hung up.

I chuckled. "Your phone skills leave a bit to be desired."

"No one has complained about them except you."

"That must be because they are all too scared to upset you," I teased.

His eyebrows furrowed. "I hope not."

He looked like he was about to disappear into a silent rumination, so I quickly changed the subject. "Do you really think that Caroline's Aunty Faith can help scrub the footage?"

"I hope so."

"The fire-starter can't be Todd, can it? Why would he show us the footage if it was him?"

"I guess there's always a chance of a double bluff or a misdirection, but I can't see how it could possibly work in his favour," Altan replied thoughtfully.

I stared out the window for a while. "Destiny seemed genuine about her situation, but you've got to admit that its suspicious that she has previous experience handling fires and didn't tell us about the loan shark earlier."

"She's told us now. Surely, she's not dumb enough to share all that and not give herself an alibi for the time of the fire?"

"Criminals are often stupid," I reminded him. "Speaking of which, I feel stupid. What do you think she meant about Clyde chasing griffins around for their feathers?"

"It seems he suffers from all types of substance abuse."

I waited for further explanation but when none came, I said, "I don't understand. What does drinking alcohol have to do with griffin feathers?"

Altan shot me a surprised look. "Oh! You don't know? Sorry, I assumed everyone knew. When griffin feathers are burned, the smoke produces a psychedelic effect."

"What? No, I'd never heard of that. So they're basically a drug?"

He nodded. "They affect some magicas more than others."

"Wait a sec. If Clyde has been smoking griffin feathers and isn't always in control of his actions, couldn't he have lit the fire?"

"Yes," Altan replied slowly. "It's possible. But how does that explain the shadow that Todd showed us from the security camera?"

A couple of pieces of the puzzle suddenly clicked in my head. "Do you realise that there's someone we haven't even considered yet?"

"And who is that?"

"Someone we haven't met yet. James, Todd's husband."

"I'm glad you're keeping an open mind, but why would the owner's husband attack the sanctuary?"

I thought for a long while then gave a defeated sigh. My puzzle pieces weren't fitting together quite as well as I'd hoped. "I have absolutely no idea."

"Maybe he's trying to steal something?"

"But if that's the case, why wouldn't he just visit Todd at work, make an excuse to go for a walk around the sanctuary and steal it while he was alone?" I replied. "Maybe he's sick of Todd being constantly stressed and working late. Maybe he wants the sanctuary to shut down."

"If that's the case, you'd think he'd do a better job of damaging the place, wouldn't you? It is still functioning perfectly fine; it just needs the claim to be paid out so that the repairs can be completed."

"Okay. Maybe my idea isn't a good one."

"Don't be like that. It's a solid idea. I'm pleased you're thinking about alternative suspects."

"Speaking of suspects, I'm going to try Lord Chatsworth again." I pulled out my mobile and took the number from Altan's contacts. This time the phone rang three times before a man answered. "Hello, is this Lord Chatsworth?" I asked politely.

"It certainly is. To whom do I have the pleasure of speaking with on this fine day?"

"It's Trix from MagicAssess. We met yesterday at the sanctuary. We're currently assessing the claim for the fire there and have a few questions for you, sir."

"Hello? Hello? Oh dear, it seems my reception is poor."

"Lord Chatsworth, can you hear me?"

"Hello? Sorry, I can't hear a thing. I'm going to have to hang up."

As the call ended, I stared at my phone before turning at Altan. "Well, if that's not as suspicious as someone wearing a balaclava in a bank, I don't know what is."

Chapter Seventeen

There was an innocent tinkle of a bell as we pushed open the front door to Faith's Emporium. Incense assaulted my nostrils as soon as I entered, and I couldn't halt a sneeze. Well, if she hadn't heard the entry bell, she'd definitely know someone was in her shop now.

As if my thoughts had summoned her, the elderly, pink-haired pixie appeared at my elbow. I shrieked and jumped backwards, landing on Altan's toes. He grunted but grabbed my waist until I steadied.

Faith pointed at us and cackled. "Hah! I told you change was coming. And what a change." She wolf-whistled at the sphinx then winked at me. "I never expected you to nab the most eligible assessor in the state."

She twirled joyfully, her purple dress ballooning out around her ankles while her tiny black shoes tapped against the polished timber floors. She was surprisingly nimble for an old pixie.

I couldn't help the blush that immediately rose to my cheeks. "That is not... I can't... He isn't..." I cleared my throat and tried again, using my no-nonsense voice. "We are not here to discuss my non-existent romantic life, Faith. We're here to investigate an insurance claim."

Obviously delighted, she clapped her hands. "Excellent. Caroline's been keeping me apprised of your career change, Trix. I'm thrilled for you, I really am. Going on a trip to Bowen for your first claim sounded like a fabulous way to start! And now I take it you're investigating the fire at the sanctuary?"

"That's correct," I replied. "We found evidence that the fire was lit deliberately to break the boundary wards, but we still don't know why. Nothing seems to have been stolen, but why else would someone want to gain access?"

"Hmmm, that does seem odd." Faith tapped her toe a few times on the floor. "I know a few of the people there. The manager, Todd, used to be a frequent customer of mine, but then he met his husband, and he had no need for my love potions anymore." She smiled.

"Love potions?" I asked.

"They're not really love potions, they just open up your heart to accepting the right person for you who may not be quite what you expected." As she talked, Faith picked up some jars of pink liquid on a shelf to our right and moved them down a shelf, ensuring that the labels faced outwards.

"The vet that looks after the sick magicas came in a couple of weeks ago looking for a healing potion for her sister." Her brows pulled together, and her voice dropped. "There was nothing I could do for the poor girl. She has a terminal illness and there's only so much magic can do."

She rubbed the back of her neck and sighed before giving herself a shake. "I also know Destiny. I believe she's the handler for the wild magicas?"

I nodded.

"She used to play netball at the Maroochydore netball courts a few years ago. A nice enough girl, although she seemed to be easily led by her peers. I haven't seen her in a long while now. Maybe she's matured."

I noted down what she'd shared on my tablet. "Thanks, Faith. That info could be helpful."

She grinned and gave a swift curtsy. "Happy to be of service! How else can I be of assistance today? I'm sure you didn't just come here for the gossip."

Altan said, "We understand that you are talented in illusion magic. I figure that goes for removing illusions as well?"

Faith glanced around the empty shop before she nodded.

Holding up the USB stick, he continued. "We've received security footage that we believe may be hiding a person of interest under an invisibility spell. Can you scrub the video of any magical enhancements to reveal who it is?"

Faith's eyes sparkled even brighter than usual as she rubbed her hands together. "Oooohhh, what a fun challenge. I can't say I've done that before, but I'll give it a good crack. Come with me."

She beckoned us to follow her and waved a hand at the shelves. "These are basic tinctures and harmless spells that some people use to try and improve their lives. They're really nothing more than parlour tricks, but the humans seem to get a kick out of them. Plus, it keeps an old woman busy and making enough money to book a cruise each year. All the really good stuff is out the back."

We had arrived at the front counter. I looked around, thoroughly confused. Was Faith losing her marbles? There was no door, just the back wall of the shop. I opened my mouth but quickly snapped it shut when she pulled a small stepladder from behind the till and dragged it toward the beige-painted wall.

Climbing up the four steps, she knocked three times on the door of a wooden cuckoo clock hanging on the wall. A hand-carved bird popped out and sat silently as Faith whispered something to it, before it disappeared back inside its home. A pink light shone from the interior of the clock before spreading out in an arch and racing down to the floor. The lines of light solidified to form a fuchsia-coloured door.

"Here we go." Faith grinned merrily as she clambered off the stepladder. "Come on, come and see!" She hurried through the doorway. We ducked our heads and followed obediently.

My jaw dropped. The space we were in was filled with floor-to-ceiling shelves of magical paraphernalia. As I tried to take it all in, I nearly knocked over an umbrella stand that held a collection of wooden staffs.

After I'd righted them, I looked more closely at a wall lined with colourful jars full of liquids and glittery substances. I narrowed my eyes at the contents: some jars were filled with things that looked an awful lot like internal organs.

I shuddered and moved my gaze to the different sized cauldrons made of various metals that were in my path. Stepping around them, I dodged the dried herbs and flowers that were hanging from the ceiling, the air heavy with their scent. On my left, sunlight streamed from the ceiling onto a giant glass greenhouse filled with plants.

"This is impressive," Altan said.

I nodded mutely, barely able to take in everything around me. He gave a soft chuckle, gripped my elbow and guided me forward. The shock of his touch pulled my focus back to the present, and I realised that Faith was getting away from us. I hurried after her, being careful to sidestep a haphazard pile of broomsticks. I couldn't hold back a snigger as I imagined Faith rocketing around town on her own flying contraption.

Seeming to read my mind, she yelled out from behind a tower of stacked boxes, "It's a common misconception. I don't use those brooms to fly. I cast a cleansing spell on them and sweep my home to remove the bad energy."

"I wonder if it works on mothers," I muttered.

"Here we are," Faith's cheery voice floated back to us. "Hurry up, slow pokes."

As we arrived at her workstation, she was spreading out ingredients on the timber bench. I didn't know how anything stayed in position because it wasn't a flat surface but a massive tree root that had taken up residence in her back room. It sprang from the ground and undulated like a snake's coils before disappearing into the earth once more.

A natural dip in the root held a stone bowl into which she was throwing various things: feathers, stones, leaves and a few drops of oil. She was chanting softly to herself. Every so often she paused and tapped her finger against her chin before snatching up something else to add to the bowl.

Eventually she announced, "That should do it, but the spell will destroy the USB stick. Is that okay?"

Altan nodded. "It's a copy of the original file. We can get another."

"Perfect." She held her hand and Altan passed it over. "Get ready. Watch the ball."

I nearly asked, "What ball?" but then I noticed a crystal ball on a plinth beside me. I was sure it hadn't been there a few seconds ago.

Altan and I drew close and stared at the centre of the sphere while Faith threw the USB into her concoction and set it alight. It flared brightly, the flame shooting a metre high. I yelped, but the sphinx's steadying presence kept me in place. "Look," he said and pointed at the crystal ball.

An image appeared. It was somewhat murky at first, but then it solidified into the security footage we'd seen earlier. How in the unicorn's mane the video had transferred from the USB to the crystal ball I had no idea. Magic was awesome.

I watched closely as the fire burned out and waited for the shadow on the ground at the sanctuary to appear. My eyes widened. There it was, but this time we could see the body that it belonged to.

The picture wasn't the best quality, but I could make out a camouflage jacket over straight-leg jeans. A wide-brimmed hat hid the person's face, but I could see a beard peeking out from under the hat. The figure paused and looked around, but kept their face pointed away from the camera. They strode swiftly in the direction of the main path and disappeared.

I hissed with frustration. Would it be too much to ask to get a positive identification from the video?

Chapter Eighteen

It was only three o'clock when we left Faith's shop, but I couldn't hide a yawn. "I'll take you home," Altan said. "This job is exhausting when you first start, not only physically but mentally as well."

"You're not wrong," I said and promptly stifled another yawn.

"It gets easier," he reassured me as he started the car and pulled into the traffic.

"I can keep pushing," I insisted. "Let's talk about the video in the crystal ball. We saw the arsonist, but we're no closer to figuring out their identity." I pouted. "It's very frustrating."

"I wouldn't say that we're no closer. We now know that they are human and male. If they were wearing a glamour, that should have been scrubbed off as well with Faith's spell."

"True, but of all our suspects that only leaves Todd. And he doesn't have a beard. The others that we've interviewed have been women or magicas. And I really don't think it's Todd... although, I've been wrong before," I said, thinking of Sylvia and the disappearing mango. "What are we missing? Do you think it could just be a random attack from a pyromaniac?"

"Don't forget Lord Chatsworth."

I gasped. "Of course! He keeps avoiding our calls. But wait... he doesn't have a beard either."

"No, he doesn't. But could he have been wearing a fake beard in case someone saw through his invisibility spell?"

"That would be clever," I said begrudgingly. Chatsworth was really frustrating me with his evasive behaviour. I stilled as a random thought flitted into my mind. "What day is today?" I asked urgently.

Altan frowned at my sudden panic. "It's Wednesday."

"Shoot, I forgot." I smacked my forehead. "I need to go home. I have to take Millie to a performance with her choir this afternoon. It starts at four."

Altan accelerated. "No problem. Do you need a lift to get there on time?"

"No, no, we'll be fine. Thanks, though." I gripped the sides of my seat as he took a corner faster than I'd expected.

Before long, he skidded to a stop in front of my house. "Thanks, Altan, I owe you," I shouted as I threw myself out of the car and ran to my front door. I turned and waved before disappearing inside.

I screwed up my face when I remembered I hadn't had a chance to return my furniture back to its usual position. Throwing my bag onto the table, I kicked off my shoes.

Before I'd even managed to leave the dining room, my mother was blocking my path, arms crossed. "Aren't we going to see Millie perform? If you want to look half respectable, you'd better hurry up and get changed," she sniped.

"What do you think I'm doing?" I asked, waving a hand towards the bathroom. "Is Millie home from school yet? The concert doesn't start until four o'clock."

She tossed her head impatiently. "No, she's not, but you need to be ready so you can help her get there on time. You do realise that Millie is supposed to arrive fifteen minutes beforehand, right? Didn't you read the note on the fridge?"

The nerve of the woman made my blood boil. Since when did she read school notes and give a modicum of concern about someone other than herself?

I squeezed my eyes shut for a second and took a steadying breath. "Okay, give me ten minutes. I'll be ready to leave by the time Millie gets home from school."

My hair really needed a wash, but I didn't have time. After a quick shower, I dressed in a simple off-white skirt and blue button-up blouse. I'd just finished pulling my hair back into a basic ponytail and was popping on a wide cream headband to hide the greasiness when my daughter burst into the house.

She tore past my door shouting, "I'm late! I'm getting changed right now then we have to leave straight away!"

I followed in her wake, stood at the entrance to her bedroom and called through the shut door, "Okay, little dove. Is there anything I can do to help?"

"I just need my sheet music – it's in the blue folder in my backpack – and a fresh bottle of water," she shouted back.

My mother appeared beside me wearing a form-fitting yellow dress and smelling of lavender. "Already got it, pet. I'll get your mum to start the car."

I blinked at the sudden return of jealousy; it felt as if a black mass of pain was sitting in my stomach. I should have been thankful that Val was giving my daughter the love and support she'd never given me, but it still stung.

Was I not good enough? Was I unlovable? Had it been my fault that my mother had never given me the emotional support that I'd craved? I shuddered. These were dark feelings, and I didn't like them. I really should book in to see a shrink now I could finally afford it. I added that to my ever-growing to-do list.

With a few more hurtful comments from my mother and a whirlwind of energy from Millie, we made it to the nursing home on time. Hurrying through the foyer, we followed the signs to a door that led us into the communal hall. Millie raced inside to join the twenty students from her choir. My mother and I followed, entering the hall just in time to see them all disappear into a side room to warm up their voices.

The nursing home's large airconditioned hall had a makeshift museum on the left with a small collection of old photos and rusty implements in glass cabinets. A small stage was at the front of the room, while rows of plastic chairs filled the rest of the hall with a clear aisle down the centre. Towards the back of the right side of the hall was a glass sliding door that opened onto a pretty courtyard. Through the glass I could see a paved walkway with garden beds filled with flowers.

A few elderly residents in wheelchairs were sitting at the front of the hall while the remainder were slowly making their way to their seats. Some younger people had joined them; it appeared that the residents' families had been invited, too.

Thinking of family reminded me that in the panic of trying to arrive on time, I hadn't thought about being left alone with my mother for an hour. I stifled a groan.

"So," Val said, awkwardly shifting her weight on her feet. "How was your day?"

I shrugged. "It was okay."

"What did you do?" she asked, twisting a ring around one of her fingers.

I frowned. Why was she suddenly interested in my day? "Just work stuff."

There was a long pause. "What are we doing for dinner? I didn't see anything fresh in the fridge, and you haven't taken anything out of the freezer to defrost."

"No. I thought we could pick up pizza for dinner."

"Come now, Trix," she reprimanded me. "Growing girls need to be offered healthy choices, not fast food."

"Yeah, like all those healthy meals that you prepared for me," I scoffed.

"Don't be rude. I did the best I could. You need to try harder."

"Freaking heck!" I hissed. "You think I'm not trying my hardest every day?"

"Trix," Val admonished as she glanced at a passing woman, "there's no need to get ugly in front of other people." It was her turn to frown. "Why are you always so angry with me?"

I stared at her incredulously. "Why am I always angry with you? How could I not be?" My voice broke.

"I don't understand why you're so hateful towards me. I don't understand what I did to deserve a child like you."

My heart shattered as the final vestige of hope that we could repair our relationship fled. "I could say the same thing about you."

"What on *earth* do you mean by that?"

All my pent-up emotions from over the years spilled out in a venomous rush. "You never let up! Nothing I do is ever good enough. You're always on my back about the way I raise Millie, or the placement of the furniture in my house, or how I could have done all these great things if only I'd tried harder. It might have been a little easier for me growing up if *you* had tried harder! I was always making excuses for you at school about why you couldn't come to events, and if I ever felt like I was finally settling into a place, you'd insist we moved again. I never had a chance to put down roots or make friends or join school teams." I was breathing heavily, and tears were threatening to spill from my eyes.

"Trix," Val spoke quietly, gripping my arm and pushing me away from any eavesdroppers. "This isn't the time or place for this conversation."

"No, no, it's not." I straightened, pulled back my shoulders and lifted my chin. The damage was done, and I couldn't stomach saying another word to my mother.

So I walked away.

Chapter Nineteen

Sitting in an empty chair on the aisle beside an older gentleman, I kept my eyes focussed on a random spot on the wall. Val could find her own seat.

"You smell sad," someone said to me.

"Huh?" I craned my neck to see who was speaking. A labrador was sitting at the man's feet; of course I was talking to an animal. I really should have expected that by now. "You can smell emotions?"

The man turned his head, and his brows furrowed over his dark glasses. "Are you talking to me, miss?"

"Oh sorry, sir. No, I was just talking to... Never mind." He made an understanding noise in his throat and faced the front once more.

"You can hear me?" The dog's tail thumped against the floor. *"Of course I can smell emotions."* It stood up and stepped closer.

The man reached down blindly, his hand seeking the dog's head. "What's up, Gavin? Why are you standing, old boy?"

Gavin leant into his owner's hand. *"You smell more sad than my John, and he can't see much of anything."*

I sighed. Lowering my voice, I said, "So, you're telling me that I should focus on the good stuff? Always look on the bright side of life and all that?"

"Of course. Is your belly full?"

"Yes."

"Do you have a safe place to sleep?"

"Yes."

"Do you have someone that loves you?"

I glanced at the front of the room where Millie was walking onto the stage with her choir. "Yes."

"Then everything else is just a possum. Pay it no mind."

I chuckled. "A possum?"

"Yes. Those brown furry creatures that sometimes visit the tree where I pee. They screech at me, and they smell funny, but I don't let them distract me from what's important."

"You're a wise dog," I murmured and sat back.

The rage from my altercation with my mother was gradually subsiding, and the sickening pit that had taken up residence in my gut felt like a pothole now rather than an all-consuming black hole. The music teacher introduced the choir, and they started their first song. My heart swelled as I watched Millie perform. I was so proud of her.

As the final note sounded, Gavin lifted his head and scented the air. *"Uh-oh,"* he said, giving a whine and nudging his owner's hand.

"What's 'uh-oh'?" I whispered.

At the same time, John said to Gavin, "What's wrong? Do you need the toilet?"

"Something's coming," Gavin said.

"What is it?"

"Something big." The dog sniffed again. *"With feathers and fur."* He gave a violent sneeze. *"And musky."*

I guessed I should be grateful that it wasn't a komada dragon this time. I leant close to Gavin's ear, realising how silly I looked to anyone who might be watching. "Can you tell me where I'll find it?"

He stood, raised a paw and pointed his nose towards the back right corner of the hall. Gavin's attention was fully focussed on the glass sliding door when his whole body began quivering. *"It is here."*

I frowned at the dog but before I could ask anything further, the sound of a heavy thud followed by glass smashing spurred me into action. I leapt up, wishing I hadn't changed out of my armour.

The sliding door to the courtyard had been smashed, and standing in the gap was a griffin. Its wings brushed the top of the door frame, while the eagle head surveyed the hall. It looked like it was looking for something. Or someone. The shocked silence was broken by screams from the audience.

"Not again," I groaned, and glanced at Millie. Her face had gone white.

I gritted my teeth and pulled my bead kit and stick out of my handbag; luckily, I had thought to pack them so at least I wasn't completely helpless. Altan's lessons about always being prepared were becoming ingrained.

I raced up the aisle to face the magica, hoicking my skirt above my knees as I did while trying not to run into people. There were more screams as the rest of the audience realised the danger they were in. If I'd had time, the slow rush to escape would have amused me. There were dozens of elderly humans using walkers and holding canes, shuffling towards the far end of the room where the choir was now rushing offstage.

Pausing in my dash, I looked over my shoulder. Catching Millie's eye, I mouthed, "Go," before blowing her a kiss.

I barely heard her yell, "Be safe!" before she was lost in the crowd heading towards the side room in which the choir had warmed up their voices.

Turning back towards the shattered glass door, I examined the magica. This griffin was a young female, smaller than the injured one from the sanctuary, but her beak and claws were no less lethal. Her colouring was a darker brown, however, her feathers were nowhere near as sleek. With random ones sticking up on her head and neck, she looked rather comical, but I couldn't let her whacky appearance lull me into a false sense of security.

Gritting my teeth and gripping my stick, I slowed down and walked purposefully across a line of now-empty chairs. As I drew closer, I pulled out a red bead: a fire attack might be enough to scare her away without having to engage in an actual fight.

The griffin squawked at me then started clicking her beak in a staccato rhythm. As I hesitated, she cocked her head, and we stared at each other for a long minute. It was quiet now that most of the humans had evacuated the room. I didn't dare look around to check who was left in case breaking eye contact sent the magica into attack mode.

I took a deep breath and the griffin mimicked me. My stick warmed in my hand and sent a feeling of safety through me. I lowered my bead. If I didn't die by the griffin's claws, Altan would kill me when he found out I'd put myself at risk on a whim.

The griffin lowered her wings and tucked them tight against her body. In response, I tucked the fire attack bead back into my bag. With a sigh of contentment, the griffin sat like a cat, curling her lion's tail around her feet.

"What in the unicorn's mane is happening?" I frowned, at a total loss.

The griffin made the strange clicking noise again as if it was trying to talk to me; too bad I could only hear mundane animals. The stick sent another surge of energy through me. I took a step forward and held out my hand, palm upwards, and instinctively dropped my eyes to the ground.

The heat of the griffin's breath blowing on my hand made me shiver. A part of me was wondering if I was about to lose my fingers when the smooth hardness of its beak pressed into my palm. I let out a shuddering breath.

"Finally."

I jerked back and dropped my stick. The griffin stayed still, watching me patiently. "Did you...? Did you just talk to me?"

She repeated the strange clicking rhythm. I picked up my stick and gingerly touched her beak again. *"There we go,"* she said, her tone relieved. *"I knew you'd figure it out eventually."*

"Why can I hear you?" I asked, incredulously. "I've only ever heard normal animals before today."

"Normal? Wow, thanks for that."

"Shoot, I didn't mean any offence. I just meant that I've never communicated telepathically with a magica before." I stared at her in wonder. This had to be in the top three most amazing – and terrifying – moments of my life.

"I figured that." She pressed her beak firmly into my hand. *"Your innate magic feels weak, but your staff is giving you a power boost."*

"I'm sorry, my what? Magic? Staff? I don't understand."

"Oh boy. And the other griffins say I'm naïve! You're like a cub who hasn't figured out their wings yet. And can you please take your hand off my face and just touch my feathers? It's uncomfortable trying to focus with you fondling my mouth."

I snorted but did as she asked and stroked her rich brown feathers. "I don't know if this clarifies things, but a tawny frogmouth told me that some of my memories had been wiped."

"Really? Well now, that would explain a lot." The griffin's eyes focussed on something behind me, and she nodded towards it. *"And what about her? Is that her problem, too? Or has she been smoking feathers?"*

"Huh?" Frowning, I turned around, my hand still on the griffin's neck. My mother had pressed her back against the opposite wall; she was clutching her chest and staring at me in horror. "Mum? Are you okay?"

She pointed a shaking finger at me. When she could finally get some words out, her tone was accusatory. "You can communicate with it?"

"With her," I corrected. Addressing the griffin again, I asked, "What's your name?"

The griffin gave a haughty shake of her head. I got the impression she was attempting to look regal, but she only succeeded in making even more of her feathers stick up at odd angles. *"My name is Geraldine. I am a member of the Sapphire flock, daughter of Richard. He is the reason I've come to find you today."*

"Her name is Geraldine," I repeated aloud to my mother. Secretly, I was enjoying getting a reaction out of her. She'd been nothing but condescending during her entire stay, so it was fun to ruffle her feathers a little. My lips quirked up. My puns were going to rival Barry's in no time.

"This can't be happening," Val wailed.

"What?" I frowned, distracted by her outburst. "So I have some strange ability to talk to animals... and to magicas as well, as it turns out. It's weird, but you get used to it."

I hadn't even finished speaking when my mother burst into tears and, gripping her handbag, ran out of the room. "Oh, fairy dust," I muttered. I held up a finger. "Sorry, Geraldine, I'm going to have to pause our conversation. I really need to speak to my mother. She's not entirely stable at the best of times, and apparently that was one shock too many." Glancing behind me at the nursing home staff who were peering out from the side room, I added, "Why don't you meet me later in private and we can talk properly."

Geraldine shook her head. *"All I came to say, was that you need to speak with my father. He has something to share with you."*

"What is it with you magicas and dancing around the facts?" I muttered. "Can you be slightly less cryptic? Where is your father and why does he want to talk to me?"

"You've met him already, but you haven't spoken. He's incarcerated at the sanctuary."

Momentarily forgetting about my mother's unexpected breakdown, I shot the griffin a look of disbelief. "Your father is the griffin at the sanctuary?" I said slowly.

"Yes." She shook her wings irritably. *"They need to hurry up and release him. He's aching to return to the skies. But he needs to share something with you first."*

I grimaced. "He's not going to hurt me, is he? I'm not sure if he told you, but it was partly my fault that he ended up there in the first place."

"Oh, skies above, no, he doesn't wish to harm you! He only wants to talk. However, I don't know what my father has to share because they chased me off before we could speak properly."

"Was it you who broke into the sanctuary this morning?"

"Yes," she replied smugly.

"Right. Well, that explains a few things. Okay, I'll speak to your father tomorrow. Right now, I have to talk to my own parent. Thank you, Geraldine. But maybe next time, you could try not to smash through glass." I released her feathers and immediately sensed the loss of our ability to communicate.

And then I did something I'd sworn I'd never do again.

I followed my mother.

CHAPTER TWENTY

"MUM!" I YELLED AS I raced through the nursing home foyer, once again lifting my skirt higher than I probably should. No doubt my mother would have something to say about my propriety when I caught up with her, but it was far easier to jog when there wasn't a skirt getting in my way. I ran through the front entrance and quickly scanned the carpark. My mother obviously didn't need to be placed in a home yet; the old bird was still quick enough to get the slip on me. Speaking of birds, I caught a glimpse of Geraldine flying into the sky as I ran towards my car.

Mum wasn't there. "Frick-a-fracking frog's legs," I snarled. I had to find her; I might not want to, but I couldn't very well leave her alone without any of her luggage. If she wanted to run away from her problems, she needed to be a grown-up about it and collect her stuff from my house first.

I jumped in my car and tore away from the nursing home before I realised that I was letting my anger get the better of me. Taking some deep breaths, I slowed and rolled down the window, then checked the side streets nearby. There was no sign of Valerie, and I was torn. Mostly, I just wanted to get back to Millie, but it didn't feel right to abandon my mother, even if it was her own fault.

Then I spotted a sign for a bar up ahead. I chewed my lip as I tried to put myself in her shoes. My mother and I had had a massive falling out and then she'd found out that I had unexplainable magical powers. It was entirely possible that she'd felt the need to rush to the nearest watering hole and numb her shock with alcohol. Parking on the opposite side of the street, I drummed my fingers on the dash as I debated with myself. I could leave her to her bad behaviour and let her figure out her own way home, but I knew that would hurt Millie.

With a frustrated groan, I grabbed my phone and got out of the car, slammed the door shut and locked it. Stomping into the public bar, I glared around at the patrons. When I didn't immediately spot my mother, I asked the barman, "Did a woman in her fifties in a yellow dress just come in here?" When he nodded, I asked, "Which way did she go?"

He pointed towards the next room, and I marched through the entrance. This area had the dining room and a second bar, and an open doorway that showed a separate room for the pokies. The sound of cheerful music and coins hitting metal as lucky gamblers were paid out could be clearly heard from the other side of the room. After studying the early dinner crowd at the tables, I hurried over to the pokies room and scanned the people sitting in front of the twenty colourful machines. There was no sign of my mother.

I was so close to using a real swear word, but before I could let loose the impending wave of rage in the form of verbal diarrhoea, a commotion back at the bar caught my attention.

A calm voice said, "Sorry, Clyde. You've had more than enough. You're cut off."

I perked up my ears at the familiar name, exited the pokies room and snuck closer to the counter. Although I kept my distance, I could see that it was indeed Clyde, the gnome who worked at the sanctuary.

"Nah, mate, you can't do that to me! The skeleton is lying." His words were slurred and even more high-pitched than usual, and he was wobbling from side to side on his bar stool.

Skeleton? What in the wolf's moon was he on about?

I drew closer, staying behind the gnome, hoping Clyde wouldn't notice me. Most of the people in this room were human, apart from the barman who was a centaur. He shook his head and clopped down to the opposite end of the bar to serve some other patrons.

"I want another drink, asshole!" Clyde shouted. "Fark you-uuu. I seen that skeleton talking shit about me. He's a wanker." And with that, he fell off his chair.

He jumped straight back up and shook his fist at a nearby potted plant. "You got a problem with me having a drink, mate? I'll rattle your bones, I will." He burped loudly. "Come on, why not have a go, then?"

Clyde was wasted. This must have been the behaviour that Todd had been talking about. I wondered if he was only drunk or if he'd been smoking feathers as well.

Suddenly he lost interest in his imaginary skeleton and wandered away from the bar, nearly colliding with some of the occupied tables as he went. With a long-suffering sigh, the centaur followed and gently guided him outside. I tailed them as the centaur bundled the gnome into a waiting taxi and gave the driver an address.

My phone rang. The number was unknown to me, but I answered it anyway. It was lucky that I did as it was Millie's music teacher asking where I was. As I gave a final glance around the bar's parking lot, I told him I was on my way back to pick up my daughter. When I hung up, there was a text from my mother.

I need a night away from you. Don't try to find me.

I blinked back the tears that immediately threatened to spill onto my cheeks. She didn't matter anymore but Millie did. I had to get back to the nursing home and put any thoughts of my mother out of my head.

Once I'd collected Millie and assured her I was unharmed, we grabbed a couple of pizzas from Terry. This time there was no sign of the druid, Falendael. I wasn't entirely sure if I wanted to see her since the last time we'd met, she'd done something to my mind, but if she had answers, I would happily suffer through another headache. When I asked Terry if he knew how to contact her, he got shifty.

"I'm too busy for idle chit-chat," he said abruptly then disappeared back into the kitchen – which was strange, considering we were the only customers in the shop. Something was going on with him, but I was too tired to push the matter.

Once we'd arrived home and dragged ourselves out of the car with our dinner, I glanced at my phone. "How in the heck is it only seven o'clock?" I mumbled. So much had happened that it felt like the whole evening was over, but only a few hours had passed since we'd left for the choir's performance.

The cheesy pizza smelt amazing. I was starving, not to mention exhausted. I felt like I could sleep for a week. I handed one of the boxes to Nicole.

"Where's your mum?" she asked, obviously noticing the distinct lack of discontented energy following us into the house.

"Great question," I muttered, before shooting a guilty look at Millie who had plonked herself on the lounge with her dinner. I moved closer to Nic and whispered, "Some stuff went down tonight. A griffin showed up at the nursing home—"

"Oh shit!" exclaimed Nic. "Is everyone okay?"

"Yes. It scared Millie, but this one wasn't attacking. Mum freaked out and took off. She texted to say she won't be back tonight. I guess she just needs to blow off some steam and then she'll come back tomorrow. I doubt she'd leave without saying goodbye to Millie." I glanced at my daughter again. "Besides, she's left her stuff here."

We were all a little subdued that night. Not even a text from Altan asking about Millie's choir performance could cheer me up before I went to bed.

Chapter Twenty-One

WHEN THE SUN BROKE through on Thursday morning, I'd already been for a jog to clear my head. I hadn't heard anything more from my mother. After a quiet breakfast with just the three of us, Millie disappeared into her room to get dressed for school. When she sauntered out in very short denim shorts and a red singlet, I stopped her.

"Little dove...I know it's free dress day today, but you still need to follow the school's uniform policy."

Millie screwed up her face. "But the girls and I planned our outfits. I won't be the only one wearing shorts."

I raised an eyebrow. "You can wear shorts...but not ones that are *that* short. And your shirt needs to be sun safe. Otherwise, you'll get pulled into the office and reprimanded. Do you want to be stuck in detention and unable to spend time with your friends?"

She gave a sullen sigh. "Ugh. Fine. I'll change." When she returned in five minutes, she was wearing a plaid skirt that almost made it to her knees and a form-fitting black top with puff sleeves.

I couldn't suppress a shiver. Millie looked so mature; she was growing up far too fast for my liking. I wasn't ready for her to leave me yet. But there were only a couple of years of high school left before she either got a job or went to university. I had a bad feeling that the next two years would speed by faster than I wanted them to.

With a hurried goodbye, Millie headed for the bus, and I got changed into my armour. Gathering my bag with my tablet, phone, bead kit, and my stick, I waited at the end of my driveway for Altan to arrive.

It was the fourth day of our investigation into the sanctuary's claim and we still didn't know who had lit the fire. If we could firmly rule out Todd, at least then the insurers would pay, but with Lord Chatsworth not responding to our calls we didn't know of anyone else who'd have motive to start the fire.

As soon as Altan arrived, I slid into the passenger seat and announced solemnly, "I have intel."

Altan chuckled. "Intel? Really? So you're a spy now?"

"Don't tease me. This is serious business." My playful tone told him I was joking.

"All right, all right. I'm sorry. Pray tell, what is this intel you speak of?"

"I talked to a wild griffin last night – the one who broke into the sanctuary yesterday."

Altan switched from jovial to shock in the blink of an eye. "You spoke to a wild griffin and you're not dead?" He scrubbed a hand over his face. "Of course you did," he groaned. "It's the fucking komada all over again."

"Stop worrying." I patted his shoulder. "I'm fine, aren't I?"

"Maybe a little insane, but physically you appear unharmed."

"Hey! I take exception to that."

He waved a hand at me. "Carry on. I'm all ears." He trained his cat-like ears forward, making himself look particularly attentive.

I stifled a giggle. "The griffin said she had a message for me."

"Did she try to kill you?"

"Nope."

"Wait a minute."

"A cotton-picking minute or just a regular minute? That's an important distinction."

He shot me a look of consternation. "What are you talking about?" Shaking his head, he didn't give me a chance to come back with a smart reply. "It doesn't matter. You said you spoke to a griffin? I thought you could only speak to normal animals?"

"She didn't particularly like it when I said 'normal animals'," I admonished him. His face twisted with frustration. "Okay! I'll stop distracting you with silly comments. It seemed like she knew I could talk to her if I used my," I hesitated on the next word, "*powers* in a certain way. I was holding my stick. I touched her and then we could chat."

"You *touched* a wild griffin."

"Yes?"

"And then you 'had a chat'." He made air bunnies with the hand that wasn't on the steering wheel then groaned with exasperation. "Fine. You're still alive. I'm going to try and stop being shocked, but I really must follow this up. I need to talk to my friends and find out what they know about people with your powers. Maybe you were dropped on your head as a baby and some magic leaked in." Ignoring my reproachful look, he rubbed a hand over his stubble then gave an explosive sigh. "Please, continue."

"Geraldine told me—"

"Geraldine?" he asked incredulously.

"Yes, the griffin's name is Geraldine. Try to keep up. Geraldine told me that her father is in the sanctuary, and he has something to tell me, so we need to go there this morning."

Altan's face paled. "Her father. The griffin that I maimed when I was protecting you and Millie? That griffin?"

"Yes," I squeaked. When he said it like that, paying Geraldine's dad a visit didn't sound like such a good idea. "I'm sure it'll be fine."

He snorted derisively. "Sure. No danger whatsoever. Oh, Trix." He ran his fingers through his hair; I was starting to think I might be the reason that some of it was turning grey. "I'll be there. I will be there so that you can voluntarily touch a griffin that has every reason to snap off your fingers in revenge."

I chuckled nervously. "It will be fiiiiine." I just wished I believed that myself.

When we arrived, Todd was on the phone in front of his office and waved us through. We left him to it and walked the now-familiar pathway. Cautiously approaching the trees that made up the fence of the griffin enclosure, I called out, "I'm here. Geraldine sent me."

A loud crashing came through the undergrowth and the male griffin appeared, looking even more imposing with every stride. He really was massive. When he clicked his beak, I cringed. That beak really could do some damage if he decided to attack me.

"I need to touch you to be able to communicate," I told him.

He strode closer and Altan tightened his grip on his sword, his bead pouch open and ready to engage.

When I tried to push my hand through the shrubbery that formed the boundary of the griffin enclosure, I hit resistance. I couldn't touch the griffin. "Oh. Oh dear." I shot Altan a look of panic.

"What is it?" he asked, his eyes tight.

I took a deep breath. "It seems that I have to be *inside* the enclosure in order to speak to him."

"Oh, come on!" Altan exclaimed before throwing his blade to the ground in frustration. Breathing heavily, he stared at the weapon for a long moment before muttering, "That probably wasn't good for it." He picked up the sword and sheathed it, then suddenly grabbed my shoulders and pulled me close to him. He stared intently into my eyes, then he sighed. "I'm doing this against my better judgement because I trust you. If there is any hint of danger, I'm pulling you out of there before you can say 'MagicAssess'. Understand?"

"Yes, sir," I replied weakly. It took everything I had not to close the few inches between our lips and kiss him. As I had the thought, his gaze dropped to my lips. "Focus," he growled. "This is serious." I wasn't entirely sure if he was talking to me or himself.

When he released me, I stumbled a couple of steps before I found my balance again. Closing my eyes, I pushed all thoughts of his mouth out of my mind. I was about to enter the cage of a wild magica whom I had accidentally helped to maim. There was every chance that he'd sent his daughter to lie to us just to get close enough to kill me. I had to keep my head on straight. To be safe, I tapped the button on my armour, letting the heavy-duty protection coat my suit like a second skin.

Fisting my hands, I focussed on my breath and blew it out slowly.

Five.

Four.

Three.

Two.

One.

Here we go.

CHAPTER TWENTY-TWO

ALTAN AND I ENTERED the enclosure together while the griffin waited imperiously for us to approach. "We mean you no harm," Altan said respectfully.

The griffin rolled his eyes, swung his stumpy tail around and waved it as if it to say, "Really?"

Out of my peripheral vision I saw Altan tense and hover on the balls of his feet, ready to strike if needed. "Hey, mate," I murmured to the griffin. "No funny business, okay?"

The magica pawed the ground impatiently, his talons ripping up the earth, then shoved his eagle face towards me. An involuntary gasp of fear burst from my lips, but when my hand connected with his feathery cheek, I could hear him loud and clear.

He was halfway through a rant. "*—believe the audacity! For you to ask me not to give you any trouble when it's your fault that I wound up losing my tail!*"

I automatically put my hands on my hips and opened my mouth to argue, then realised I couldn't hear him anymore. With a frustrated sigh, I returned my hand to his face.

"If anyone needs to be scared of me," the griffin continued, *"it's that sphinx of yours."* He glared at Altan. *"I loved my tail."*

I tried to reason with him. "Look, mate, you can't blame us for trying to protect ourselves and the people around us at the netball courts."

"Stop calling me 'mate'. My name is Richard. And it was your fault."

"Why do you keep saying it's my fault? You're the one that burst out of the bushes and started screaming. We all thought we were going to die!" I chided him.

Meanwhile, Altan looked like he was about to explode from worry. It must have been difficult not being able to hear one side of the conversation when the magica might decide they wanted to kill you at any second.

"I would never have done that if it wasn't for your friend."

"My friend? What are you talking about? Altan only reacted to your threat."

Richard stomped a talon. *"Not him! That damned druid! She asked me to go talk to you, and when I said no, she messed with my mind. It was not an acceptable use of her talents."*

"What druid? I don't know anything about this. Who asked you to talk to me?"

"What druid?" Altan parroted and looked at me. I held up a hand to shush him.

"All you druids have weird names. Her name was something like 'full-on-dial'."

I pursed my lips as I thought about the name. My eyebrows raised when I realised who he meant. "Do you mean Falendael?"

"That's the one." Richard gave a self-satisfied shake of his feathers.

"I've only met her once! She's certainly not my friend. I don't understand."

Richard lifted his wings in his version of a shrug. *"Well, you'll have to talk to her about it. That's all I know."*

"Was that what you wanted to tell me? Was that the reason why you sent your daughter to find me?" I asked.

"Oh, no, that was just a side note. I've been watching you two blunder around here investigating the fire for the past four days and figured you needed some assistance."

"Do you know something about it?" I asked.

"It was lit with magic," he replied, his tone distinctly superior.

"Yeah, we've already figured out that much. Did you see who caused it?"

He harrumphed. *"You'd better treat me with the respect I deserve, otherwise I'm not going to talk to you anymore."*

I gave a long-suffering groan. "Fine. Oh, great and mighty Richard, who has blessed us with his presence today." Altan raised an eyebrow, but I pushed on, knowing how ridiculous I sounded but not caring. "Please, oh wise and exalted one, grace us with your wisdom and share the secrets that you so fiercely protect."

"Now you're just being facetious," Richard complained.

"I don't know what you want from me!"

He stared at me for a long moment, and I stared straight back, issuing a challenge. To my surprise, he threw his head back and laughed. In doing so, his movement dislodged my hand, and then all I could hear was shrieking.

Altan immediately went on high alert and raised a bead. "Don't bother," I grumped and folded my arms. "He's laughing."

Shock coated the sphinx's face. "You're telling me that you made a wild griffin, whose tail we amputated, laugh out loud? Maybe I should stop underestimating you with magicas."

"I keep telling you not to worry about me. You just need to listen better," I scolded.

The griffin shoved his face back at me, his eyes alight with merriment. *"You amuse me, child. I shall help you."*

"I am so glad," I replied sarcastically.

"I wish to share something with you that I noticed shortly after the fire."

"I'm listening."

"Once the unnatural fire had broken the boundary wards, I sensed someone at the fence. I could not see them, but they smelt human. I believe there may have been magic covering their physical appearance."

"We've actually figured that one out, too, but it's good to have a first-hand account. Thank you. However, we still can't figure out what they were doing inside the sanctuary or their identity."

"I'm not sure how useful it is, but I do know one thing."

"Go on," I urged.

"The intruder crept past my cage—"

"Cage," I interrupted with a scoff. "This is more like a resort than a cage!" I swept my hand out to indicate the grassy paddock dotted with shrubs, trees, and flowers, not to mention the fresh-water creek running through the middle of it.

He glared at me. *"When you are used to the joy of winging through the unlimited sky, this is indeed a cage."*

I cocked my head; that was a valid point. "Fair enough." I raised my hands in submission. "Sorry if I offended you."

"Do you want me to tell you the story or not?"

"Yes, I do. Please."

He gave a self-important sniff. *"Then please stop interrupting."*

"Certainly, sir. Please continue."

"As they snuck past me, I saw their shadow. Once they'd gone upwind, I could no longer smell them, but I could track that shadow. It went that way." He used his wing to point towards the stables.

"Into the stables?"

"Yes. I heard a commotion with the unicorns."

"With the unicorns? What sort of commotion?" I asked.

Altan demanded, "What happened to the unicorns?"

"Just wait. I'll tell you everything when I can," I said. "What happened then?" I urged Richard.

"The unicorns have been sick ever since the fire," he said. *"I am unsure if it is related, but they were unwell the following day and now two have crossed the Rainbow Bridge: the sire and his unborn colt."* He bowed his head sorrowfully. *"I am unsure if the person responsible meant to kill them or if it was an unfortunate side effect of whatever they did."*

"Thank you, Richard. That is extremely helpful. Is there anything else you can tell me?"

He paused thoughtfully. *"They came out the same way that they entered. Their emotions were a strange combination of shame and hope."*

"Thank you very much. And we *are* sorry about your tail."

He harrumphed and broke the connection before loping away.

"Holy forking shirtballs," I said to Altan, my eyes wide. "We have to go and talk to the unicorn."

"That was the most painful conversation I've ever listened to," he protested. "I am *dying* to know what he said to you. Put me out of my misery!"

As I quickly relayed what Richard had shared, Altan finally relaxed his stance and zipped up his bead kit. He pressed the crystal in the tree trunk and the gap opened in the trees once again, allowing us to pass through. "That's excellent. Let's see what the unicorn has to say before we speculate further."

We hurried over to the stables but stopped in the breezeway when we saw Anna and Becky in the unicorn's stall. Becky was holding the mare's halter and stroking her cheek while the vet drew blood from her neck. The unicorn was upright, but she was swaying a little on her feet.

Altan clicked his tongue sympathetically. "She's still not herself?"

"No, she's not," Anna responded softly. "I'm doing everything I can but it's not enough. I've got to take this vial for more tests to try and figure out how to help her."

"I'm sorry to hear that," I said. "I hope you find the answers soon."

"Thank you," Anna said as her sister removed the halter from the unicorn's head.

Keeping to Altan's suggestion not to reveal my knowledge of my magic, I went on, "Don't mind us, we're just getting out of the heat of the day to write some notes. We're not in your way, are we?"

"No, you're fine," said Anna. "We're finished here anyway. Just keep your noise to a minimum, please. She needs rest."

"Thanks. Will do," I whispered. I pulled out my tablet and busied myself with writing notes. Altan followed my lead and buried his nose in his phone.

Out of the corner of my eye, I saw Harrison, the carpet python, slither across the breezeway. He paused and raised his head, looking at us as his tongue flicked in and out. *"Nice to sssee you,"* he hissed a greeting. *"Honey's here again."*

"Hey, mate. Good luck with the rat hunt," I murmured.

Harrison gave me a hard stare and flicked his tongue out again, before slithering away. I wished I could ask him if he saw anything during the fire. But I didn't want to risk the sisters hearing me holding a conversation with him and figuring out my secret.

Five minutes later, Anna and Becky packed up their medical equipment and left. As soon as I was sure they'd gone, I put my tablet away, pulled out my stick and let myself into the stall.

"Hey, girl," I soothed. "I'm just here to have a talk."

I took a deep breath, then hissed it out slowly through my teeth. Gripping my stick, I hesitantly reached out to the unicorn.

Her eyes were half-closed and appeared vacant, although her skin shivered at my touch. The stick sent its now familiar wave of energy into me, and I leant into its power.

"Hi there," I whispered. "I'm Trix. I'm here to help. What's wrong with you? I might be able to get you the right medicine if you tell me what's happening."

The unicorn gave a heavy sigh but didn't respond. I prodded the connection between us, unsure how to encourage her to speak to me. "I should be able to hear you if you try speaking to me," I said gently. "Did something happen to you after the fire? Did someone come here?"

She gave a pained grunt, but the connection remained silent. My brows pinched together, and I shot a worried look to Altan. "Something isn't right. I can't hear any thoughts from her. I don't want to push it and risk exhausting her."

"It's probably for the best to leave her be. I would hate for us to cause more harm in the pursuit of the truth," he said. Worry coloured his tone as he studied the magica.

"I wish I could make you better," I murmured to the mare as I leant my forehead against her neck.

I needed to figure out what happened here after the fire – and fast. I had a strange feeling that the unicorn's life depended on it.

Chapter Twenty-Three

EVEN THOUGH THE DAY felt like it had gone on forever, it wasn't even lunchtime when we drove back to head office in Brisbane City. We were discussing the latest developments in the claim as Altan found a space in the basement carpark beneath the MagicAssess building. "Everything is pointing to Chatsworth," Altan stated as he pulled on the handbrake. "It has to be him."

"I reckon you might be right," I said and opened my door. "And remember the conversation we overheard between him and Todd? He really wanted that dead unicorn's body, and he was fuming when Todd said it was going to the university."

"If only he would answer our phone calls." Altan gave a frustrated sigh as he shut his door with a little more force than necessary. "Why don't we blow off some steam? We haven't had a chance to start your Brazilian Jiu Jitsu training yet. How about we have a session now while Caroline recharges your armour?"

I was still learning my way around MagicAssess, so I obediently followed Altan as he took me straight to Caroline. When we arrived, he waited outside her tiny door, while I ducked into her workroom and changed into tights and a singlet that I kept packed in my oversized handbag. Leaving my armour with the green-haired pixie, who promised to have it back to me before the day's end, I returned to Altan and together we took the elevator down a floor to the training level. Altan drilled me on my magica knowledge the entire way. "If a harpy attacks you, what do you do?"

"Block your ears, run like heck and pray to whatever God you believe in that it doesn't catch up."

He smirked. "Pretty much. There are ways to fight a harpy, but most rely on a hefty supply of beads and having at least one other person with you. And if you've finished reading that book you borrowed, you'd know why that is. Can you remember?"

I scrunched up my face as I recalled the textbook's warning. "They have lethal talons that easily cut through bone and sinew. Their scream can paralyse you, they have a dozen loose feathers on each wing that act like throwing knives, and their bite is venomous."

"Very good."

I didn't have long to preen at Altan's praise before he raised his eyebrow and asked, "And how *should* you deal with a spider weaver if there are no helpful trees around?"

I chuckled weakly. "With their ability to create illusions, it's best to nullify their magic as quickly as possible. If you don't have void-cuffs on hand, you can use a bead to create a bubble around you to stop the magic that affects your mind. Unfortunately, the effect doesn't last long, so you must work quickly to incapacitate the weaver. As we saw in Bowen, when a spider weaver is knocked unconscious their illusions stop working."

"Well done." He looked impressed. "And what about a basilisk?" he asked as he opened the training room door and gestured for me to enter first.

"A basilisk?" I wracked my brains. "They look a bit like a giant snake, right? I don't think I've read much about them yet. Are they related to the komada dragon?"

"A cousin. I want you to go back to the library this afternoon, find a book on reptilian magicas and study up."

I groaned. "I can't this afternoon, sorry. I've got to take Millie to netball practice and I also..." I exhaled slowly and squeezed my eyes shut, "I need to find out whether my mum came home today."

Altan opened his mouth, shut it again with a clack, then he said, "You failed to mention that. Is everything okay?" His voice was filled with compassion.

I wrapped my arms around my torso. "Not exactly. Val has been rubbing me the wrong way all week and last night I finally blew up at her. But that's not the worst part." I steeled myself, unsure of how he would react. "She saw me talking to Geraldine." At his blank look, I clarified, "The griffin that came to the nursing home."

"Wait. What nursing home?"

"That was where Millie's school choir performed yesterday."

"I see. So your mother saw you communicate with the griffin? What did she say?"

"She totally freaked out and ran off. All she had with her was her handbag."

"Are you worried about her? Do you want to lodge a police report?" He stopped and put his arm around my shoulders. For once, my body didn't react like a hormonal teenager; it just felt nice to be comforted. "I can come with you if you need support."

I shook my head. "It's fine. Mum texted me and said she needed space, so that's what I'll give her." I shrugged, pretending her rejection hadn't cut me to the quick. If I didn't think about it, maybe it wouldn't hurt so much. "Please, can we talk about something else?"

He gave me a squeeze then removed his arm. "If that's what you want. Make sure you check out another book on magicas as soon as you have some free time. Are you still exercising every day?"

"Almost. Sometimes I go for a jog in the morning before anyone else is awake. Other times, Millie and I have been jogging in the afternoons. She wants to improve her fitness for netball, so we've made the effort to go together on days when she's free. She's been making me do sprint intervals, too," I grumped. "I've never scowled at my own child more than I have in the past week."

Altan chuckled. "What a good kid! Tell her she's got two thumbs-up from me. Make sure you keep increasing your distance as it gets easier. But you need more than just fitness – when it comes to fighting magicas, you need to be multi-skilled. I want you to start practising your archery and swordsmanship on alternate days, either here or at home. Plus, I want to teach you how to turn your body into a weapon when you don't have one to hand."

"Huh?" I wrinkled my face as I tried to understand what he was saying.

"We need to get you training in hand-to-hand combat. Like I said in Barry's office on Monday, I have training in Brazilian Jiu Jitsu, so we'll start there today. As you get stronger, I'll get you to seek out competent trainers in other hand-to-hand fighting styles so that you continue to expand your abilities. The good thing about BJJ is that it teaches you where the weak points are on a body when you're locked in a hold. All the sword training in the world is no use to you if someone heavier than you has pinned you on the ground and you don't know how to break free."

"I remember in high school we were given a self-defence lesson by some random guy. Aren't I meant to smack my hands over their ears to burst their eardrums or something?" I mimed placing my hands over my ears.

"That's a good plan in theory, but does it work in practice?"

I cast my hands wide and shrugged. "Well, I don't know, do I? I've never had the opportunity to—"

Before I could finish my sentence, my whole world was thrown off balance. Moving lightning fast, Altan grabbed my wrists, tugged me forward to get me off balance, then swept my feet from beneath me. I landed on my back with a *whump*, the air in my lungs momentarily knocked out of me. Seriously, MagicAssess needed to invest in crash mats for their training room.

While I gasped like a fish out of water, Altan sat on top of me.

He.

Sat.

On.

Top.

Of.

Me.

If I hadn't been so busy trying to drag oxygen back into my lungs, it would have been the most erotic thing that had happened to me in years.

Sad, I know.

He waited a moment until I'd caught my breath then dragged my hands over my head. As he pinned them there, his eyes drew level with mine. I gulped. My brain was frizzing out and I had zero coherent thoughts in my head.

"Trix." There was a warning note in his voice. "Focus on me, please."

There wasn't anything else I *was* focussed on, that was the problem. "I am." I tried for indignation, but it sounded closer to a moan. This wasn't fair.

"Does your self-defence lesson work in this scenario?"

"What lesson is that?" I was having trouble thinking straight because all I was concentrating on was not letting my traitorous body react. Not that I would have ever admitted that to him.

"Can you burst my eardrums from the position you're in?"

I struggled weakly against his hands, trying to wiggle my wrists free, but that just made everything feel even more intense. For me, anyway. The sphinx seemed unphased by my squirming.

"I'm going to teach you how to get out of positions like this. Hopefully you'll never need to know, but better to know it and not need it than the alternative, right?"

"Sure thing," I whimpered.

Concern flooded his face, and he shifted his weight off me. "Am I hurting you?"

"No. I just... You're so... It's been a long..." I huffed an exasperated sigh. "Don't worry about it, just hurry up and get the lesson over with."

"Oh. *Oh*!" Altan looked startled for a moment before a devilishly mischievous smile lit up his face. "I think I understand."

I was mortified. A part of me desperately hoped he didn't understand because that would be simply too embarrassing. Another part of me hoped that he did and that he would stop the lesson in the interests of reducing the unprofessional amount of sexual tension fizzing in the air between us. And another very small part of me hoped that maybe he felt the same way, that maybe he would close the gap between us and finally let me taste his lips.

To my distress, Altan neither ended the lesson nor kissed me – he made it even worse. He continued teaching me while knowing full well that my brain was currently residing in the gutter.

While I lay on my back like a dead fish, gasping for air, he released my hands and moved to a new position kneeling between my knees. Grabbing my calves, he hoisted my legs up to wrap them around his hips. "Lock your legs around me, Trix," he practically purred.

I did as instructed, unable to look away from his glorious face. Frick-a-fracking mother trucker. What a tosspot. This was far too close, far too intense. Not that I didn't want to feel his body between my legs, but there was no way I could remain cool and professional when the object of my desire was exactly where I'd imagined him in my fantasies.

Altan gripped the front of my shirt right above my breasts. This was better than any of the romance novels I'd read. "This is the guard position," he continued. He couldn't know that the blood pounding in my head was drowning out his voice. "It's actually a great position for you to be in because there are plenty of sweeps and holds you can use to get out."

He placed my hands in various positions and had me move my hips and knees to demonstrate how to escape. The final move had me groaning... and no longer in a good way. "I'm thirty-five. My hips aren't that flexible anymore!" I yelped.

He leant forward and whispered in my ear, "Try for me, Trix."

How dare he use my lust against me? Taking advantage of him being off balance, I grabbed his shirt and clumsily tried to replicate one of the sweeps he'd shown me. I threw my weight upwards and twisted. It wasn't smooth or pretty, but he was so surprised that he didn't put up a fight. I managed to flip him on his back so that now I was sitting astride him.

"Ha! I did it!" I crowed at him, raising my fists in triumph.

His hands rested lightly on my waist and the touch of his fingertips started a blazing fire in my core. He smiled up at me, looking more handsome than anyone had any right to be.

Oh no, this position was far worse.

CHAPTER TWENTY-FOUR

Staring down at his beautiful face, I thought about all the ways I could make him mine. My insides turned to jelly, my breathing hitched, and my heart rate skyrocketed. I was done for.

And then Altan's phone rang. Of course it did.

I scrambled off him and stood up as he pulled his flip phone out of his pocket and answered it. Suddenly he was all business again, despite still lying on his back on the floor.

"Ros?" he said, then paused while the other assessor spoke. I couldn't make out what she was saying. "Are you okay?" He listened intently and sat up, his tail flicking with agitation. "I'll be right there." He hung up and stood.

"What happened? Is she okay?" I asked.

"She's been hurt on a job, and she needs me."

"What can I do to help?"

He gave me a soft smile. "Nothing. I'll take care of it. You drive my car home and find your mum. I'll collect it tomorrow."

"Are you sure? How are you going to get to Ros?"

He shrugged. "I have my ways. Don't worry about it. But I really do have to leave now. Drive safe. I'll let you know what's happening tomorrow, as soon as I'm free." He handed me his keys and left the room.

I suddenly felt empty. His absence had left a gaping hole in my chest, which was ridiculous. I saw him most days, and now that he was giving me the afternoon off, all I could do was mope about how much I was already missing him.

A small sprig of jealousy pushed into my stomach, and I felt slightly sick. Why was he going to Ros? I needed him, too. In my heart, I knew I was being unreasonable, and I felt frustrated and ashamed of myself. *Of course* he had to help his colleague; she was in trouble. It might have boosted my ego if he hadn't gone to her, but he'd have gone down in my estimation for not helping a friend in need.

Ugh.

And all that rationalising did no good at all. I knew I was being illogical, but it didn't stop that little seed of jealousy desperately trying to take hold. I pushed it away. Feelings were dumb.

I'd only managed to get lost twice inside MagicAssess when I went to collect my recharged uniform from Caroline. I then drove straight to the netball courts in Maroochydore to pick up Millie from her team practise. She got the surprise of her life when she saw Altan's fancy black car. Her big eyes turned to me, a question already forming on her lips.

"Don't get used to it," I said quickly. "Altan loaned it to me because he got called away. We're giving it back tomorrow."

She gave a playful pout then started an in-depth recount of her training session. "By the way, Nanna came and watched for a bit. She said she wanted to see me play because she can't stay to see my game on Saturday."

"You saw Nanna today?" I asked, my voice accidentally going up an octave.

Millie nodded then eyed me curiously. "Yep. I take it you didn't know she was coming? Or that she's leaving today?"

"No, I haven't been able to get a hold of her." I tried very hard not to show Millie how hurt I was that my mother hadn't spoken to me. I'd tried calling her, but I'd only got her voicemail, and she hadn't replied to my messages.

It was time to shove all that pain back in a box, nail it shut and shove it far into the recesses of my mind. I had Millie, I had Nic, I had Altan. I didn't need anyone else.

By the time we got home, I'd managed to put my feelings aside… but I had also stiffened up from my first Brazilian Jiu Jitsu lesson. Feathers and fur, but all that tussling on the floor had been hard work!

After I'd hobbled out of the car and into the house, I went straight to Millie's bedroom. Standing in the doorway, I could immediately tell that my mother had collected her things. There was no sign that she'd ever been there. I breathed a sigh of relief. At last, the house could return to some sort of normalcy.

When Nic arrived home, I enlisted her help to move the furniture back the way it had been before my mother had swooped in and changed everything. Millie hid in her room and worked on assignments.

After eating dinner together, I checked my phone. There was a text from Altan.

> Dear Trix, I forgot to tell you, I have something for you in the boot of my car. Sincerely yours, Altan.

Greetings, sir. This is a polite reminder that you don't need to use formal speech in texts. While you consider your repeated blunder, I shall examine your vehicle and locate this mysterious package.

No need to be cheeky. Let me know once you've opened it.

I will. But first, is Ros okay?

She'll be fine. I await your report on my package.

Unsure if the subtle innuendo was deliberate or not, it didn't stop me sniggering to myself. With curiosity and excitement bubbling in my chest, I raced out to his car. The parcel was probably something boring and work-related and I'd feel disappointed once I opened it. But why would he be so secretive if that was all it was?

I pulled the flat, square box out of the boot and returned to my bedroom. I hesitated before opening it, my hands trembling a little. Taking a deep breath, I undid the red bow and lifted the lid.

My first impression was of warmth. The rich brown and gold folds drew a gasp of admiration as I fingered the expensive fabric. I wasn't much of a clothes aficionado, but I knew enough to recognise quality.

Carefully lifting the garment out of the box, it took me a moment to sort out the various layers but when I did and they fell into place, I couldn't stop a moan from escaping.

This. Dress. Was. Glorious.

The gorgeous chocolate-coloured corset, puff sleeves, sweetheart neckline, full layered skirt and multiple hidden pockets, all combined with a gold choker, had me swooning. Maybe I was a clothes person after all.

I picked up my phone. How could I even start to communicate my gratitude for this?

I typed quickly.

I opened it.

And?

I absolutely love it. Thank you!

I knew Caroline had your measurements, so I had her make it for you for the ball.

You didn't need to ask her to do that.

Oh, don't worry, I paid her for her time.

You paid for this to be custom made…for me?

Yes. I hope you like it. Plus, it has a similar type of protection built into it as your usual armour. The button to activate it is hidden in one of the puff sleeves.

It's amazing. Thank you. I didn't really have anything decent to wear to the ball. I was going to try and find time to go shopping before Friday.

You do realise that the ball is tomorrow night?

I knew that.

Of course you did. Changing the subject, have you heard from your mother?

Yes. She's safe but she's left town.

I'm sorry to hear that. Are you okay?

My fingers hovered over the phone as I debated typing that I was fine. I wasn't, not really, but it wasn't a conversation I wanted to have over text.

I'm managing. We'll talk about it another day.

Okay. Try and get a decent night's sleep. Tomorrow will be a big day. Good night, Trix.

Thanks, Altan. I truly appreciate your support. Good night.

I connected my phone to the charger then turned back to my beautiful dress. I couldn't quite believe it was mine. With a reverence I'd never felt for any piece of clothing before, I stroked the fabric before hanging it carefully on a clothes hanger. Altan had had this made especially for me. There was no way that I wouldn't be wearing it to the ball, even if I looked ridiculous in it.

CHAPTER TWENTY-FIVE

AFTER DROPPING MILLIE AT the bus stop, I drove to Bards and Beans where Altan had asked me to meet him. He was standing on the kerb holding two takeaway cups of coffee. He hopped into the passenger seat and passed me my oat latte. I took a sip, the dragon-frothed oat milk hitting my tastebuds in the perfect way, then carefully placed it in one of his cup holders.

"Sorry about yesterday," Altan said.

I refused to let yesterday's patch of jealousy show. "That's fine. Is Ros okay today?"

"She will be. Barry found a good healer for her, so she'll be right as rain in a week or two. She did have something interesting to share, though."

"What was that?" I asked as I merged into a turning lane.

"There's been another fire close by. Ros was planning on moving to that claim next, but I'll take over to take the strain off her. She's sending the file to me this morning. I'll log in shortly and check it out. I don't know if the fires are connected."

"You said it was close by. How close are we talking?"

"About twenty kilometres. A car was burnt out."

"That doesn't sound relevant. Why do you think there may be a connection?" I frowned as I accelerated.

"Because the claim for the damaged car was lodged by Destiny."

It took me a second to realise he was talking about the person and not fate. "Oh! That does sound dodgy." I tapped a pattern on the steering wheel as I thought about it. "But wait, we saw that the arsonist was a man in the video. Why are we circling back to Destiny?"

"We only saw the beard. The camo jacket was bulky enough to hide a...womanly figure." He cleared his throat.

"Are you actually considering that the beard might have been used as a disguise?"

"I'm very frustrated by this claim but yes, I'm keeping an open mind. That means that I can't discount the female suspects without further proof that it was a man."

"But why would Destiny burn her own car?"

"Maybe she lied about the loan shark. Maybe she's playing the victim, and she destroyed her own car in an effort to look innocent. She gets paid out for her car and... I don't know." He heaved a frustrated sigh. "It's just another theory. For the record, I still think its Chatsworth, but I have no hard evidence linking him to the crime."

"So where are we going now? Am I going on the highway to the sanctuary?"

"Not yet. I want to pin down Lord Chatsworth first."

Altan tried calling him again, but it went straight to voicemail. It seemed like the sanctuary's patron was avoiding us. Why?

I pulled over and we switched places. As Altan drove, I finished my coffee while I found the lord's social media accounts on my phone and looked him up on my preferred search engine. A few newspaper articles popped up about his work with the Magica Sanctuary of Queensland and his early life in England. They were mostly positive, apart from a report about his house being broken into the previous month when a water kelpie's hide and a kapamu's skull were stolen.

Staring at the screen, I pondered for a minute. I decided to look him up again, but this time on our internal system through my tablet. Result! Dave's assessor files had a claim for Chatsworth. I sucked in a breath and held it as I started reading the file. The claim had been denied the previous month due to attempted fraud.

"Altan?" An edge crept into my voice as a loose theory snuck into my thoughts. However, I wanted to hear Altan's thoughts first before I got ahead of myself.

"What is it, Trix?"

"Chatsworth. I just found something about him on MagicAssess's system." I read out the information.

"Well, blow me down." He gave a low whistle. "Maybe that explains why he doesn't want to talk to us. But has he struck again? Or is it something else?"

"Why would he strike again? He's a philanthropist: he just provides funding to keep the sanctuary operating."

"The one time we spoke to him, he seemed keen to have us pay out the claim. Maybe he went in to steal a rare artifact that he knew Todd wouldn't give him and was feeling guilty about the damage."

I laced my fingers and leant back in my seat. "That would make sense." I squeezed my eyes shut and rubbed my temples. All this speculating was tiring.

Altan spoke again. "Let's figure out where Chatsworth is and confront him."

Using the information from Dave's file, it didn't take us long to locate Chatsworth's home address. It was nearby and we were there in minutes. The mansion had an intimidating security gate and high fences.

We buzzed the intercom at the entrance. Altan introduced us then said into the speaker, "We wish to speak with Lord Chatsworth. Is he at home?"

A man with a Welsh accent replied; it wasn't Chatsworth but his butler.

"Who even has butlers these days?" I muttered. Altan's eyes crinkled but he didn't respond.

"I'm afraid not, sir," the butler said politely. "He is at his office today."

"Where is his office? It's a matter of urgency and we can't get a hold of him on the phone. We need to speak with him now."

"His office is in Capalaba, sir, although I fear he may have appointments all day. But his receptionist should be able to point you in the right direction."

Altan got the address and thanked him before reversing out of the driveway. Fifteen minutes later, we'd reached the bustling business precinct of Capalaba, but it took us another five minutes to find a parking spot.

Finally, we located Chatsworth's office on the second floor of a three-storey building. The pretty young woman at the front desk looked at the sphinx in surprise but greeted us warmly. "And how can I help you today?"

After a glance at Altan, who indicated I could take the lead, I introduced us both. "We're here to see Lord Chatsworth."

She frowned. "Do you have an appointment?" She looked at her screen and clicked a few times, her frown growing deeper. "I can't see you listed."

"No, but the matter *is* urgent. We need to speak to him today and he hasn't responded to our phone calls," I said.

"That's odd. I'm afraid he's not available – he's in an offsite meeting – but I'll see if I can get a hold of him. Just one moment." She made a call but received no answer. "I'm so sorry for the inconvenience. He's flat out preparing for a charity ball tonight.

I'll be sure to let him know you popped by. You should try again on Monday. He'll be in the office until lunchtime."

Altan and I shared a glance. The charity ball; as a major patron of the sanctuary, of course Chatsworth would be there.

"Thank you so much for your help." I flashed her a genuine smile then spun on my heel and left the office with Altan right behind me. Once we were back in the car, I turned to him. "What do we do now?"

"We track down Chatsworth at the ball." Altan ran his fingers through his shiny dark locks. "And we should let Seargent Barracks know our concerns. He may want to place a man at the ball to make an arrest if it's necessary."

"That's a good idea." I nodded, then yawned.

"Look, why don't I drop you home? I've got a few jobs to do today. Among other things, I want to check out Destiny's insurance claim to make sure it's not connected to the sanctuary fire. I can see how drained you are, especially with everything that's happened with your mother, and we've got a big night ahead of us. If I take you home now, you can get some rest and prepare for the ball. Does that sound like a plan?"

"I don't want to abandon you to do all the hard work!" I exclaimed.

"But you won't be. I'll call as soon as I figure out what happened with Destiny's car, and you'll be rested and ready if shit hits the fan tonight. Make sure you stash your bead kit in one of the dress's pockets and wear comfortable shoes."

He certainly knew how to please a woman, that was for sure: he'd asked me to wear comfortable shoes *and* given me a dress with pockets. "Thank you again for the gown. It's the most beautiful dress I've ever seen."

Was that a blush on Altan's cheeks?

"Good," he replied gruffly. "I'll take you home now and meet you there tonight. Remember lesson one?"

"Expect the unexpected."

I had a feeling tonight's event was going to throw me some curveballs. I just hoped I was ready to catch them.

Chapter Twenty-Six

Ellie had messaged to say she would pick me up at six o'clock. I made sure I was ready on time, having enlisted both Nicole and Millie to help me with my hair and make-up. Once Nicole had finished with my face, she stood back to admire her handiwork. "Damn, girl! You look smoking hot."

I smiled, a little embarrassed. "Thanks, Nic. What do you think, Millie? It's not too much, is it?" I waited anxiously as my daughter studied me from head to toe.

After rearranging a wayward curl, she grinned. "You look amazing, Mum. Not exactly how I'm used to seeing you, but I love it." She hugged me, being careful not to smudge my make-up or crease my gown. Checking the time, she said, "You'd better get out the door. Ellie will be here any minute."

I picked up my phone and checked the screen. There'd been no new messages since Altan had called earlier and told me that Destiny's report had been truthful. During the afternoon he'd found the loan shark, who confirmed they'd set her car on fire. The cold edge in his voice had made me wonder if he'd taken justice into his own hands.

Once again, all roads were leading to Chatsworth. Hopefully, tonight we'd finally find out if he was involved.

I was excited about seeing Altan so we could discuss his afternoon's work in more detail. Obviously, there was no ulterior motive in seeking his company... it wasn't like I'd been missing him. After all, we'd only been apart for a few hours.

After slipping on my ankle boots, I tucked my phone, driver's licence, house key and bead kit into my deep pockets. Anticipation of the unknown was making my hands shake and my heart race. I blew out a deep breath.

A toot from the front of my house made me jump. "Time to go. Don't wait up," I joked. With one last hug from both Millie and Nic, I raced outside.

Ellie had arrived in a sleek black limousine. My jaw dropped as the driver opened the back door and my elven friend emerged.

"You look absolutely stunning," she said, kissing my cheeks in greeting.

"So do you!" I exclaimed, in awe of her flowing silver floor-length gown.

"Psshh! There'll be twenty women there who look just like me, but everyone will be talking about you. Where did that dress come from? It fits you like a glove." She stroked the skirt, as enamoured by the rich fabric as I was. I couldn't resist giving it a little swish. It really was perfection.

I slid into the back of the limo before answering, "Altan had Caroline from work make it for me. She already had my measurements, so it was no problem."

"You didn't even have a fitting?" she asked incredulously.

"No. When I was first measured, Caroline used this magical tape that seemed to have a mind of its own. It was... disconcerting, to say the least."

"Oh my," Ellie placed a hand over her heart. "Sentient tape that remembers your measurements? Now that's the best idea I've heard this month. I must tell Vic." She opened a small door in the passenger console to reveal a glass bottle and two crystal flutes. "Champagne?"

Technically I was working, but surely one wouldn't hurt? "Yes, please. Is Vic coming tonight?"

"Not tonight, I'm afraid."

"That's a shame."

"Speaking of partners," Ellie went on, "I wanted to ask how your date with Perry went?" Her eyes were alight with curiosity.

I hesitated. "Erm. Well, you know how awkward first dates can be."

She gave a tinkling laugh. "That's true. Poor Perry was so nervous when he called me to get your address – he'd completely forgotten to ask for it when you accepted his invitation! And you say 'first dates', so I'm hoping that maybe there'll be a second one?"

"Oh. Umm, I don't know. I'm still finding my feet with my new job, and Millie is really busy with extracurricular activities at the moment. I'm not sure how much time I can give him."

"He seems pretty invested in pursuing you, so I wouldn't stress too much about him losing interest due to your schedule. I'm sure you'll figure out a time that works for both of you." She smiled happily.

Perry was her brother, and I didn't have the heart to tell her that he wasn't a good fit for me. We spent the rest of the ten-minute drive catching up, while the driver slid smoothly through the traffic.

When we arrived at a grand hotel in the middle of Mooloolaba, Ellie explained, "I donate a small amount of money to the Magica Sanctuary of Queensland every month, but one of the other patrons, Lord Reginald Chatsworth, owns this place. Every year,

Todd holds a charity ball to raise money for the sanctuary, and every year Chatsworth books out his hotel for the event at no charge." She leant closer to me and lowered her voice, "This is pure gossip, but I did hear on the grapevine that Chatsworth is an old flame of Todd's. People say that he continues to support the sanctuary in the hopes that they will end up back together. Personally, I think Todd and James are smitten with each other, so I don't believe there's any chance of that."

I raised my eyebrows. "I had no idea that a magica sanctuary could hold so much drama. It's like a flipping soap opera!" Another idea occurred to me: if it was true that Todd and Chatsworth used to be an item, then I couldn't help but wonder whether the lord would do his ex's bidding if Todd asked him to set a fire. That could be a very compelling motive. I filed that thought away to discuss with Altan at some point tonight.

Once we'd both gotten out of the vehicle, the limousine disappeared around the corner and another fancy car immediately took its place. Dozens of beautifully dressed people were making their way up the steps of the heritage-listed building. As I followed suit, I gawked at its opulence. There were marble columns covered in thousands of twinkling lights standing like sentinels beside the arched entrance. A red carpet ran up the steps with enormous urns filled with giant bouquets of pale exotic-looking flowers on either side. And that was only the outside.

I gripped Ellie's arm and said, "This is amazing. Thank you for inviting me."

"You're doing me a favour," she replied generously. "I didn't really want to come alone tonight. Thank *you* for accepting my invitation." She patted my arm.

Walking me up the red carpet, she pointed to our right as we entered the grand old building. A unicorn made of ice was cantering around us, its hide glittering like diamonds. It tossed its head, reared, then trotted over to greet another newcomer. That was some impressive magic. I looked around for the source of it and saw a wizard near the front door, controlling the life-like ice sculpture.

Beside him, a handsome blond man was leaning against the wall trying hard to appear nonchalant. I smiled surreptitiously at Sergeant Barracks; I really hoped we could catch Lord Chatsworth and get a confession from him tonight. Barracks caught my gaze, and his eyes widened slightly as he took in my appearance.

Not wanting to arouse suspicion by chatting with the police, I looked up – and gasped. An illusion of a rainforest canopy filled the ceiling. Following the line of the branches across the ceiling, my eyes travelled the length of the extravagant ballroom to a waterfall streaming down the far wall. The tinkling sound of the water hitting a small indoor pond provided a serene background noise that was enhanced by the string quartet that was playing on a raised dais beside it. Waiters glided through the hall serving hors d'oeuvres while a massive champagne tower sat in the centre of the room. I wasn't used to events as elegant as this one. Nervously, I fingered the button on my puff sleeve, reminding myself that I had magic armour hiding in the dress if the proverbial poop hit the fan.

All my worries vanished when I located Altan. His dark emerald-green suit had been tailored to fit his body perfectly. Forgoing a tie, he'd left the top button of his crisp white shirt unbuttoned and my imagination ran wild at the thought of what I wanted to do to that small strip of bare skin. I shuddered, frustrated at my lack of composure and tried to rein in my desire. This was not the time or place.

Altan's eyes scanned the room. Before I could ogle any longer, he met my gaze and strode over. "Good evening, Ellie. Good evening, Trix." He gave a small bow. "Sorry to interrupt, ladies." He held out his hand to me. "May I have this dance?"

I gulped. My insecurities were screaming at me not to showcase my clumsy footwork in front of the three other couples who were already dancing and the dozens of spectators. I shoved my misgivings into a box and slammed the lid down hard.

"I'd love to," I replied airily. Only someone who was paying close attention would have noticed the quiver in my voice.

Altan swept me onto the dance floor and immediately took the lead. He stopped scanning the room and held my gaze. His hand was on the middle of my back and my skin warmed at his touch. I tried to keep my body separated from his, not wanting to cross any lines, but he dragged me close and pressed his hips to mine. "This is the correct position," he whispered.

I whispered back, "I don't know how to dance, not like this… though I might be able to do a basic heel-toe line dance." A nervous giggle escaped my lips.

His smile was dazzling. "Don't worry." His breath tickled my ear. "I've got you."

The string quartet on the raised dais played a fast-paced three-beat melody and I somehow managed to keep my feet. Thank the wolf's moon Altan was a good dancer because my knees were shaking, and my legs felt as if they might give out at any second due to a combination of nerves and muscle fatigue. Note to self: do not attend a dance in the same week that you train in Brazilian Jiu Jitsu. I almost stumbled when the music swelled and Altan swung me into a spin.

In any other company, he would have far outstripped the expertise of most men. However, this crowd was mostly elves. Was it a prerequisite that non-humans should be able to waltz?

The dance ended with me feeling rather breathless from being held so closely for two whole minutes. I automatically made to step away, but Altan didn't release me. "Another?" he asked, cocking his head.

My heart squeezed at the sight of what I thought was hope in his eyes. There was no way I could say no to him. "Of course." I prayed he couldn't hear the tremble in my voice.

I felt completely out of my depth amongst the graceful elves, and I didn't understand why Altan was looking at me in that way, but I wasn't going to sabotage whatever our relationship might be working towards. I couldn't let my lack of confidence and fear push him away. And bully to my worries about a taboo workplace romance! If he decided to choose me above other women who were clearly so much more his equal, I would take that blessing with two hands and never let it go.

The next song started and this time the music was slow and haunting. Altan pulled me even closer. As he bent his head to mine and our cheeks touched, I felt sure my heart would burst. "Are you enjoying yourself?" he asked. The smell of his cologne was heady and intoxicating.

I took a deep breath before realising I'd waited too long to respond to his question. "Best night of my life," I tried to keep my tone light.

He gave a soft hum of contentment as he squeezed my hand, and I wondered if sphinxes ever purred. His tail reached over his shoulder and gently brushed a loose strand of hair away from my face. "I'm very glad to hear that," he murmured.

This felt almost like our sparring sessions but with a lot less aggression. As I moved with him, I felt the same familiar patterns that we fell into during training, but instead of blocking punches I could focus on the feel of his muscles and his fingers laced through mine.

It was only because we were so close that I noticed tension sneak into his body. The next moment someone cleared their throat behind us. "May I cut in?" a familiar voice asked.

Dazed and blinking, I automatically complied and pulled away from Altan. He resisted for a moment before releasing me. "Peri-adonus," he said formally and gave a curt nod. "If the lady has no objections."

"Perry!" I exclaimed. "I didn't know you'd be here." He looked very smart in a crisp black suit and bow tie, and I gave him a friendly hug.

"Trix!" He held on to me a little longer than was necessary. "May I have what's left of this dance?"

I glanced at Altan and felt my heart fracture a little at the cold indifference that I now saw on his face. While I generally avoided confrontation, I couldn't give Perry what he wanted; thankfully I had a good reason to refuse without hurting his feelings. "I'm sorry, Perry." I glanced around then whispered, "Altan and I are working undercover tonight. We have to stick together."

Perry blinked in confusion and looked between the sphinx and me. "Ah. I see. Sorry. I'll leave you to it."

He disappeared into the crowd and Altan pulled me back into his arms. Resting his cheek atop my head, he whispered, "Thank you."

We danced in silence for another minute. As we twirled around the dance floor, I started taking notice of the other guests. Ellie was talking to Todd and a satyr, whom I assumed was his husband, James. James was still an enigma to us, and I wondered what he thought of Chatsworth's continued attentions to his husband. The next person I recognised was Clyde; he was sitting by himself with a drink in his hand, staring sullenly at a female gnome in front of him. Even the sisters, Anna and Becky, had dressed up and seemed to be enjoying themselves as they watched the ice unicorn perform a piaffe on the spot. The faces swirled around my brain as we spun, leaving my thoughts even more confused than before. We were still no closer to an answer. Sure, we had our suspicions, but nothing concrete.

While we danced, Altan whispered in my ear, "I haven't had a chance to tell you yet, but I was mulling over your comments about James this afternoon. I ended up chatting with Caroline after you left me and she mentioned that she was jealous we got to meet

James." At my confused expression, he chuckled and said, "That was my reaction as well. Apparently, James is a well-known star on an app." He scrunched up his face. "I think it's called Tickety Tok?"

I chuckled, "Close enough."

Altan grinned. "Anyway, I looked into it, and he was running a livestream on Tickety Tok at the time the fire was started. Most of his audience is in America so he keeps odd hours. There's no way he lit the fire."

I breathed out a sigh of relief. Not that I knew James, but I was glad for Todd's sake that his husband hadn't committed arson.

I realised then that Altan was surreptitiously guiding us closer to Lord Chatsworth. He must have spotted him standing near the pond, talking animatedly with Destiny, and decided to catch him unawares. His plan didn't work. Unfortunately, Chatsworth noticed us and excused himself, slinking away through the throng of people.

Altan cursed under his breath as we broke apart. I'd gathered up my skirts ready to make chase, when someone else caught my eye. "You!" I hissed.

Lord Reginald Chatsworth would have to wait.

CHAPTER TWENTY-SEVEN

ALTAN WAS ON IMMEDIATE alert, whipping his head back and forth so quickly I feared he was going to pull a muscle. "Who?"

"Falendael," I snarled softly. "I'm sorry, but I'm leaving Reginald to you. That druid has a lot to answer for and I can't let her disappear. I'll be back."

I stomped towards her in a very un-ladylike fashion. She looked stunning. Her floor-length gown was made entirely of leaves, and her wild black hair had been tamed back into a messy plait that snaked down her back. "We need to have a chat," I said abruptly when I reached her.

Her haughty indifference quickly warmed to amusement as she recognised me. "I wondered when you'd figure it out." She laughed before glancing around. "I'd love to talk, but not here."

She turned and whispered in her companion's ear, and he shot me a quizzical look before returning his attention to the couples who were dancing. Falendael glided towards me and took my arm. She guided me away from the dais and into a quiet hallway.

Once we were alone, she said, "Okay, I'm ready. Hit me with it."

I opened and closed my mouth a few times. How did you start a conversation with the person who had completely changed the course of your life? Finally I spat, "You...you...you did this to me on purpose, didn't you?"

She watched patiently as I spluttered. "And what, pray tell, is 'this'?"

"You meddled with my head so I can talk to animals."

"Ah. That. Yes, well, I didn't mean to. If I'd known you were my kin, I wouldn't have gone near your pretty little head. However, I do find you an intriguing mystery."

"Woah, woah, woah! Let's rewind a bit. Now I'm more confused than ever. Your kin? I don't understand what you mean."

"Well, you see, my dear," she spoke slowly, like I was a five-year-old, "when we met at the pizza shop, your plain appearance led me to assume that you were just another human. That night I was a little frustrated with some other unrelated events that had been pissing me off, so when you got in my way I decided to send some of my magic to you. Just for fun, you understand. I needed to blow off some steam. It wouldn't have hurt a normal human, just made them feel a little confused for a few hours," she assured me quickly. "You should have been fine. But you're not a normal human."

I gaped at her. "What do you mean I'm 'not a normal human'? I *am* a normal human – or at least as normal as humans ever are. You're the one who gave me weird powers."

Falendael laughed in my face, which immediately got my back up. "No, you're not. You must have druid ancestry because otherwise there's no way you could speak with animals. I was confused when I connected with you and sensed the difference in your head. You obviously have some sort of untapped druidic power, but it felt unusual. As a test, I sent the griffin and the komada after you.

Not to hurt you, you understand," she added hastily when she saw the anger on my face. "It was just to engage you in battle and force you to use your magic. But after the griffin, I realised that maybe you needed some help. If you'd never gone through any of the druid rituals, you might not have the ability to communicate with magicas like the rest of us, so I sent the komada with a gift for you.

"When they come of age, every druid asks The Giving Tree for a boon. The tree presents them with a branch to act as their staff to help them control and grow their magic. I sent the komada with your gift from the tree. You're welcome, by the way."

Was she talking about my stick? "But...but..." I spluttered, overwhelmed by the infodump. "I didn't ask for this!"

"You should be thanking me for stepping in. You might have gone insane if I hadn't unlocked your power. Once I was in your head, I could sense it bubbling under the surface with nowhere to go, like a blind pimple. It would have gotten more and more painful for you if I hadn't lanced it."

I wrinkled my nose. "That is a gross comparison. But I can't be a druid. You guys have all that other Earth magic, like growing the sanctuary's trees into fences and stuff. I can barely keep a plant alive."

"Has your garden been looking healthier lately?"

"Well, yeah, but I just thought—"

"You thought wrong. Your latent magical ability will keep the plants around you alive and healthy. Some of us are blessed with specific talents: for example, I'm very skilled at using plants as weapons in combat. My brother is a gentler soul, and he enjoys shaping plants like the ones you saw at the sanctuary. He likes to use them for protection rather than as weapons." She rolled her eyes, as if the thought was ridiculous. "You seem to be particularly attuned to communication, though it must have been frustrating to have limits on how you could communicate with wild magicas.

I'm glad you figured it out on your own. Good job, sport." She gave me a jovial pat on the shoulder.

"How do you know what I've been doing since we met?"

"I have my ways of keeping an eye on you," she said with a secretive smile.

I fixed her with a hard stare. "That's called stalking."

She rolled her eyes again. "Whatever. However, a word of warning. Druid-human hybrids are not exactly common. If I were you, I'd keep this knowledge a secret for now. There are people who will try to take advantage of you."

I frowned. "How secret is 'secret'? Surely I can talk to Altan about it? And my daughter, Millie? It's her heritage, too."

Falendael placed a hand on my forearm and looked at me sternly. "Seriously, I wouldn't. At least not until we have more answers." She glanced over her shoulder towards the ballroom. "The fact that your ability had been locked away tells me that someone important in my world really didn't want you to know about your power. If you trust the wrong person, you could put yourself or your daughter in danger."

I chewed on my lip; she'd made a good point. "I can trust Altan. He would never do anything to hurt me or Millie."

"Perhaps not intentionally, but he might talk to someone whom he thinks holds the answers for you and, in doing so, condemn you to being locked up and used as a science experiment. Do me a favour and keep your mouth shut, okay?"

"Fine," I growled. "I won't say anything for now,"

"Good girl," Falendael purred. "Now, why don't we return to that glorious champagne tower? It is nowhere near big enough, but if I'm going to be with humans all night I need as much help as I can get."

With the bombshells she'd just laid on me, I would need a drink or two as well. When she made to leave, I grabbed her arm. "I will definitely have more questions. What's your phone number?"

"Ugh. Phones are nasty things. If you need to talk to me, just ask the trees. I'll visit you when I can."

"Ask the trees? What the heckin' heck does that mean?"

She shot me a withering look that told me she thought I was a big dummy. "Precisely that. It's not that hard."

I was readying myself to argue when a voice from the ballroom called for everyone's attention. I groaned in frustration. "This isn't over."

"I'll look forward to our next meeting," Falendael replied and gave me a cheery wave before sashaying out of the secluded hallway and disappearing into the crowd.

CHAPTER TWENTY-EIGHT

THE GUESTS HAD ALL gathered in front of the raised dais. As the murmuring of the crowd lessened, the ice unicorn pranced up to the waterfall. It reared, pawing the air, then leapt into the water. As its magic hit the spray, the ice burst apart and turned into thousands of snowflakes that drifted out over the hall. The stunning display drew a collective gasp of awe from the audience, followed by a round of applause. Todd stepped up to the raised dais then, tapped the mic and cleared his throat. He looked unusually stylish in a tuxedo, and it was the first time I'd seen his strawberry-blond hair slicked back. As the crowd hushed, I scanned the room for Altan, but I couldn't see him – or Lord Chatsworth, for that matter. I gave up my search and focussed my attention on the formalities.

After welcoming the guests, Todd listed the magicas the sanctuary had saved and released back into the wild that year, then urged us all to give generously. He was just reminding us about the charity auction that would begin shortly when the sound of someone retching interrupted him.

I looked to my left and saw young Becky doubled over, hurling her guts up on the floor. Hurrying over to her, I dropped to my knees to see if I could help. Anna was beside her, too, holding back her hair as she continued to vomit. "What's happening, Becky?" she begged. "I don't understand."

Her sister's skin had grown ashen as the pool of vomit grew larger, and blue lines were spreading across her pale skin. As she passed out, Anna managed to catch her before she hit the floor and carefully moved her away from the mess.

"Someone call triple zero!" I snapped.

I'd done a basic first-aid course the previous year, but even so I didn't really know what I was doing. Wracking my brain, I placed Becky into the recovery position and checked her mouth for obstructions. Next, I took the pale woman's wrist and checked her pulse. Her heart was still beating, but it felt weak. She looked terrible.

Anna stared at her sister, tears running down her cheeks. I turned to her. "There's no time to think about this from a personal perspective, Anna," I said abruptly, trying to break her out of her panic-induced freeze. "You're a vet, you know stuff about bodies. What's going on with her?"

"I don't know," she wailed. "This shouldn't be happening."

"I know she's your sister, but I need you to focus." The stress in my voice made me sound cold, even to my own ears. "Could she have taken something?"

I shook Anna's arm, forcing her to focus her attention on me. "Don't worry, Becky won't get in trouble, but we need to know what to tell the paramedics once they arrive." Standing up, I yelled, "Is there a doctor here?" Surely there had to be one doctor at a posh charity ball?

"I am!" a voice called from the back of the room.

I returned my attention to Anna. She was no use to anyone in her current state. As the doctor knelt beside Becky, I dragged Anna upright and pulled her away. Her head dropped forward onto my shoulder, and she whispered, "This is all my fault."

As her long hair tickled my nose, the smell of honey-scented shampoo hit me, and I made a hundred connections at the same time. I froze as everything clicked into place. It made sense but I still couldn't believe my own logic.

My hands gripped Anna's arms tightly. "Faith told me," I whispered. "Harrison even gave me a clue. And I never saw it."

Anna froze before removing her face from my shoulder, her eyes filled with guilt.

"Faith said you came to her shop looking for a cure for your terminally ill sister, yet I've only ever seen Becky looking healthy. Until tonight, that is," I watched her, wondering if she would confess. She remained mute. "Harrison mentioned 'honey'. I thought he was just giving me a nickname. But he was referencing the smell of your shampoo." At her blank look, I remembered that she wouldn't know who Harrison was since I was the only weirdo who spoke to snakes. Giving her shoulders a little shake, I said, "By the wolf's moon, Anna, talk to me."

She stared at me for a long time as some sort of battle raged behind her eyes, then defeat took over and she crumpled. I held on to her to stop her hitting the floor. "Tell me everything." I was pretty sure I knew what she was going to say.

"Unicorn blood," she whispered to me and covered her face with her hands in shame.

"You lit the fire to get to the unicorns?"

"Yes," she whispered. "But it was all for my sister. She's dying. The university ran a trial with unicorn blood which was very successful, but Becky was placed in the control group, and they never treated her with the actual blood." She dashed tears from her eyes. "I had to take matters into my own hands to save her."

I sighed, my heart hurting for the two women. "I'm sorry." I squeezed her hand.

"It feels good to finally tell someone. I never said anything to Becky, just told her I'd bought a new magic medicine to try. It was making her feel better and she was so happy." She hiccoughed. "I'm not sure how much you figured out, but you may as well know everything.

"I used a fire spell to break the fence and its protection wards, and an invisibility glamour to gain access to the sanctuary. I wasn't sure if it had any special illusion-removing wards, so I also wore a disguise. I figured if anyone saw me, they'd assume I was a man. I took two vials of blood from the unicorns and injected them both with a special sedative that should have made them drowsy so Todd would call me in to treat them the next day. My plan was that I would keep coming back and taking small amounts of their blood to administer to Becky. With a mysterious illness, it wouldn't have been unusual to see me taking blood for testing. If I could keep giving them small injections of the sedative at the end of each visit, it would make them appear unwell for a longer period of time, guaranteeing me a long-term supply. But I must have gotten a bad batch of the sedative because the stallion died, and the mare lost her foal. I never meant for that to happen."

She covered her face with her hands. "All that suffering, and for what? Becky's body is rejecting the blood." Tears were dripping off her chin and I pulled her in for a hug.

There was a commotion at the entrance to the building as two paramedics arrived with a stretcher to take Becky away in the ambulance. "I have to go with her," Anna sobbed.

Altan appeared beside me. When I'd explained everything to him as quickly as I could, he looked at me incredulously. "You mean to tell me we arrested the wrong man?" He laughed harshly. "And on top of that, you tell me that the right man is actually a

  A. L. TIPPETT

woman who was trying to save her sister? Sometimes I hate this job."

I spoke softly, "We're not the police. We could just let her go."

"We need to make the report," he said slowly. "But I guess we don't need to make the arrest."

I shrugged. "If she wants to hand herself in or go on the run, that's her prerogative."

The sphinx studied me for a moment then, to my surprise, he chuckled. "You're very good at encouraging my bad habits."

He whispered something in Anna's ear and a fresh wave of tears spilled onto her cheeks. When she opened her mouth to speak, he held up a finger. "Don't say a word. It's your choice what you do with your life."

"Do you promise—?" she started.

He cut her off. "Yes. My word is my bond. I'll make sure Becky gets the best care, whatever you decide to do."

Anna nodded. "I'll go with her to hospital. Once I know what's happening to her," her voice hitched, "I'll hand myself in to the police." She looked up at the dais. "I'll have to tell Todd. I don't want him to find out through the newspapers. He was good to me, and I broke his trust."

She grabbed both mine and Altan's hands. "Thank you for this," she whispered. With a final watery smile, she left us.

"Should we tell Barracks that we have the wrong man?" I asked Altan when Anna was out of earshot.

He stretched up his arms and yawned. "You know what? Reginald pissed me off by not answering the phone. He can get charged for obstructing an investigation and have a sleepover in the holding cell, and we'll let the police know tomorrow. Plus, that gives Anna time to do the right thing."

I grinned. "Okay. That works for me."

He pulled me in for a hug and I breathed in his scent as I melted into his embrace. "Well done," he said quietly. "You found the truth all by yourself. I'm proud of you."

Chapter Twenty-Nine

I COULD HAVE STAYED in that position forever, but all too soon he pulled away. "Why don't we call it a night?" he asked. "We've done our job."

Suddenly bone-weary, I nodded.

We drove back to my house in comfortable silence. "Thanks for dropping me home," I said. "Did you want to come inside and talk some more?" I blurted it out before the butterflies fluttering in my belly filled my throat.

"Sure," he responded lightly, and I wondered if anything ever ruffled him.

I was overjoyed that he'd accepted... and horrified as I remembered the state of my living room. Why hadn't I taken the time to tidy up before I left the house? I unlocked the front door and turned on the kitchen light. "Excuse the mess," I said breezily, pretending that I didn't care that someone I admired would witness my slovenly ways.

He snorted. "You should see my place. Mess doesn't bother me. And you're a busy woman! Honestly, there's no need to apologise."

Warmth flooded me at his easy acceptance, but then I found a new problem to worry about. "I'm afraid I don't have any alcohol in the house. Nic might have some wine stashed somewhere, but I dare not get between her and her go-go juice."

"I don't need alcohol to enjoy my evening," he murmured.

Another shiver ran down my spine at what he was insinuating but I ignored it and opened the cupboard. "I can make you a tea, a coffee or a Milo."

"A what now?" he asked.

"A Milo. You know, like the cat in *Milo and Otis*."

"What cat? What's Milo and Otis? Are we consuming a cat?" He looked horrified.

Geez, Altan really needed to get out more – or rather, stay in more. "Never mind the cat. It was a movie reference. Don't worry about it. Milo is a sort of a chocolate and malt drink from an Aussie company. It's usually marketed for kids, but I won't deny that I like drinking it on cooler days. I suppose it's a bit like a hot chocolate, though it tastes different."

Altan's tail curled. "Well, I do love a hot chocolate, so I'll try your Australian version."

"You can drink it hot or cold. Which would you prefer?"

"What's your favourite?" he countered.

I grinned. "In my opinion, four heaped teaspoons in cold milk are perfect."

"Four?" he exclaimed.

"Hey, it used to be four heaped *tablespoons*. I've cut back."

He heaved a sigh. "All right, fine. I'll give it a go."

I chucked the brown powder into my favourite mug with a flamingo on it and poured the milk in, sneakily glancing at the expiry date to make sure I hadn't forgotten to replace it. There were still a few days until the date printed on the side, so it was all good. I gave the drink a light stir – what was the fun in having a cold Milo if you didn't eat some of the delicious powder floating on top?

I handed it to him with the spoon still in it. He looked at it then looked at me, his brows pulling together in a comical mask of confusion. I mimed spooning it into my mouth and a surprised chuckle escaped his lips. Obediently, he scooped a spoonful of the powder into his mouth and chewed. His face didn't give anything away. He then removed the spoon, licked it, and raised the mug to his lips. As he drank, his eyes closed, and he gave a soft moan of pleasure. When he lowered the mug, he had a milk moustache. I couldn't stop the giggle that burst from my lips.

I clapped a hand over my mouth as his eyes flashed to mine. "Sorry." I stuttered over my words. "It's just...you've got... Here." I ripped off a piece of paper towel from the roll and automatically reached over the counter to wipe his face.

He reached up and grabbed my wrist, stopping me mid-wipe. A flash of electricity swept through my body, and I caught my breath. My heartbeat started thumping loudly in my ears.

His pupils had dilated so they almost consumed the amber irises, and his tongue flicked out and licked his lips. I noticed a flash of an elongated fang that made me gulp. With his free hand, he put down the mug then stepped around the side of the kitchen bench and pulled me closer.

"Trix..." he whispered my name, his lilting accent now so familiar to me and so very precious.

I couldn't speak. I could only watch, mesmerised as his gaze held mine.

His tail wrapped around my waist and held me in place as he closed the gap between us. He released my wrist and raised both of his hands to cup my face.

"I have fought this attraction in vain. I know I am your superior at work, and policy dictates that we should not get involved. Not only that, but a sphinx and a human—"

He shut his eyes for a moment. When they opened again, they were burning with a fierce hunger; he looked as if he could devour my soul. "But every day you find ways to exert your hold on me more deeply than I ever imagined possible. I cannot deny my feelings any longer. If you don't care for me in the same way, please tell me now."

I stared at him, dumbstruck, unable to believe that he felt the same way that I did.

His eyes continued searching mine. "Trix, say the word and I will never broach the subject again. I know how it must seem, a sphinx infatuated with a human, and a colleague at that. It is not the done thing. You may even find the idea repulsive." He turned his anguished face away.

"No." I put my hands up between his arms and took hold of his face, forcing him to look at me. "Altan! Repulsive? Never." My voice husky, I finally spoke my truth. "I adore you."

A smile slowly spread over his lips and amazement coloured his tone. "You adore me?"

"Honestly, I'm surprised you didn't realise. I didn't think I'd done a very good job of hiding my feelings."

A bubble of joyous laughter burst from him. His tail tightened around my waist, and his chuckles subsided as quickly as they had begun. One of his hands wound under my tumble of hair and he wove his fingers through my locks. "I've wanted to do that all night," he said with a sigh. "Your hair is glorious."

My heart swelled. No one had ever complimented my hair, let alone called it glorious.

With his free hand, Altan held my chin and tilted my face up to his. He paused, waiting to see if I would draw away, but instead

I surprised both of us by rising on my tiptoes and meeting his lips with my own.

His shock melted away swiftly, and he deepened the kiss. His lips moved feverishly against mine and electricity crackled between us as he tightened his embrace. I ran my fingers through his dark hair and moulded my body against his. My nerve endings were firing a thousand messages throughout my body, fireworks were exploding behind my eyelids, my stomach was performing back-flips, and my skin was tingling where our bodies connected.

His fingertips dragged down my spine and I gasped. I had never felt like this before; in that moment there was nothing else in this world that I wanted more than him.

Much to my distress, Altan pulled away. Dropping his fore-head to mine, our heady breathing mingled together. "Trix," he moaned.

The lust was evident in his voice and a thrill raced through me that I had caused it. His eyes were closed, and a tremor ran across his shoulders. He cleared his throat and opened his eyes, gazing at me like he was seeing the sun after the longest night of his life. "Please stop. I want to do this properly."

I stared at him in horror. "Oh bollocks. Don't tell me you believe in abstinence before marriage?"

He threw his head back and guffawed. I'd never heard him laugh like that and I loved it.

Once he'd recovered from his bout of merriment, he replied, "No, that's not what I mean. I was serious about what I said about work. We have our entire lives to spend together and to explore each other's bodies. Let's talk to Barry on Monday about what we need to do to have this relationship signed off officially, so no one can make any complaints."

I blew a raspberry at him, resulting in another chortle. Rolling my eyes, I acquiesced begrudgingly. "Fine. Plus, Millie is asleep down the hallway and I'm not sure how quiet I will be after such a long time. I don't want to scar the poor girl."

He laughed again and I couldn't help joining in. "Don't worry." He stroked my hair. "It's difficult for me to wait too, but it will be worth it in the end." He nuzzled my neck then kissed me tenderly, sending another fizz of sparks through my body.

"Not as difficult as it is for me," I grumped, burying my face in his shoulder.

"Not true, although I might be better at hiding it," he murmured. With a sigh, he added, "I should go now before I change my mind."

I peeked up at him hopefully. "You know, you are allowed to change your mind."

He gave a deep chuckle. "I shouldn't."

He released me and I suddenly felt cold. My heart gave a pained thump. This man was something else. "I miss you already," I said, feeling like a petulant child but unable to stop the words.

He grinned. "I think that might be impossible. I haven't even left yet."

"It *is* possible. I can feel it." I rubbed my chest.

"Text me any time. I'll see you again soon, I promise. I probably won't last until Monday either." With a kiss on my forehead, he said, "Goodnight, sweet Trix. Dream of me."

CHAPTER THIRTY

SATURDAY MORNING CAME AND went in a blur. Over an early breakfast, I shared the details with Nic and Millie of the glamourous evening I'd enjoyed, then attended Millie's netball game while catching up with Ellie. I had to admit to myself that my head wasn't really focussed on the conversations with my loved ones. Altan's romantic confession the previous night was all I could think about.

When Ellie asked if Perry had contacted me to arrange another date, I dodged the question. I simply didn't care for Perry romantically. He was a lovely man, and he was rich and generous. Any girl would be lucky to catch his eye... but he wasn't meant for me.

Altan was my world. He was the only one I waited to hear from every day, the one whose approval I craved. The one who brought a smile to my lips by just being there. When I was with him, it felt like I was finally home. There was no pretending, no games, no being anyone other than myself.

Sure, he pushed me to better myself, but I relished the challenge. There was no need to contort myself to fit into the box of who he expected me to be. I felt like I might burst from all the love that was waiting to spill over the walls I had built up over the years. I was finally happy.

I had to tell him.

When Millie opted for a sleepover with Isabella, I gave a silent cheer. I called Altan, planning to ask if he was free for dinner that evening. When he didn't answer, I left a voice message and waited impatiently for him to respond.

Half an hour later, he texted to say he could meet me that afternoon for an hour in the library. It wasn't exactly what I'd had in mind, but anything was better than nothing.

I drove there joyfully, even managing to arrive fifteen minutes early. As I wandered the shelves, studying the titles of magica biology books that I hadn't had a chance to borrow yet, an older lady approached me and introduced herself as one of the librarians. "I've got a sphinx by the name of Altan waiting to speak to you in one of the conference rooms. This way, please."

I followed her, curious as to why he'd invited me to a private room instead of finding me among the shelves. She let me into the room then shut the door behind her. Altan was facing away from me.

"Hey," I said softly. Something seemed off but I couldn't put my finger on it.

He gave a laboured sigh and turned almost reluctantly towards me. "Hey, Trix."

I hesitated. "Is everything okay?"

"Take a seat." He gestured to one of the chairs.

I sat down and waited for him to do the same. He sat opposite me, our knees almost touching, but he refused to meet my eyes. What had I done wrong?

The silence hung heavy between us. "I need to know something," he finally said.

"Of course. You can ask me anything." My brow furrowed and I leant forward, placing a hand on his knee.

He grimaced and gently removed it. An icy hand gripped my throat as the fear of rejection reared its head. "I need to know the truth. Do you already know how you can communicate with animals and magicas?"

I froze. Falendael had been very clear that I should keep the revelation about my heritage to myself, that it was a matter of safety for Millie and me. But this was Altan: how could I lie to him?

I hesitated a beat too long before saying, "I don't know how to answer that."

He bowed his head and took a deep breath. "So you know but you won't tell me. Is that right?"

Panic was setting in. My heart was beating a staccato rhythm against my rib cage while a pit of despair had taken up lodgings in my gut. "Last night, I spoke to Falendael. She gave me some sensitive information, but she told me not to share it wi—"

"With me?"

"With anyone."

He took another steadying breath and squeezed the bridge of his nose. "Someone called me this morning. They didn't identify themselves, but they told me you were part druid."

Relief flooded me. He knew my secret already, so technically I wasn't going against Falendael's advice. I relaxed a little. "According to Falendael, that's correct." I watched his face closely, waiting for the acceptance and warmth I knew were coming.

Except they didn't come.

It was as if shutters had closed over his eyes. He leant back in his chair, as if trying to distance himself from me. "And you're sure of this?" A flicker of desperation flashed across his face before he shut it down.

He looked like a stranger. Hurt bloomed in my chest, but I shoved it away. There had to be a satisfactory explanation. "I'm not sure of anything anymore, but the facts fit. Why? Please tell me what's going on?"

He gritted his teeth. "Do you know that druids can control magicas? How can I trust my own feelings for you? How can I know that you're not manipulating me?"

"Because I would never do that." I hated how small and broken my voice sounded.

His hands tightened into fists. "I'm sorry, Trix. I have to protect myself. I need to leave." He stood, walked past me and then hesitated, his hand gripping the back of my chair as he swayed.

He cast one look over his shoulder at me, his gaze full of pain and longing and hurt. "Stay safe," he whispered, but then he was going through the door, and I was alone.

How had it come to this?

I made my way to my car on autopilot then started driving in a haze, not really aware of my surroundings. As usual, the radio was on in my car, but I was barely listening to it. The clock struck the hour and the introductory jingle for the news came on. The usual reporter greeted the listeners and opened with her first report.

"Police have advised the public to stay vigilant after an escaped prisoner attacked a tech store employee in Kawana Waters earlier today." My ears pricked up; I hadn't heard anything about this, and Kawana Waters was only a twenty-minute drive from my house.

"The spider weaver charged with stealing the Big Mango in Bowen escaped custody yesterday. The police officer on duty claimed that dark magic was used against them. The magica is considered armed and dangerous, and the public should not approach him. Anyone with information as to his whereabouts is encouraged to call Crime Stoppers."

My blood turned to ice in my veins. The last time I'd met the spider weaver, he'd tried to kill me and nearly succeeded. The only reason I'd survived was thanks to my stick and help from a tree. I had no idea how to replicate the power that had filled my body that afternoon, plus I was in a city now. What if there were no trees to help when he attacked?

My breathing escalated and my throat closed as I imagined him showing up at my house and grabbing Millie. He wouldn't do that, would he? There was no reason to hurt my daughter. But murderers weren't logical.

I realised my hands were shaking on the steering wheel, so I indicated carefully and pulled off to the side of the road. My head felt fuzzy. What if he came for me? I moved the driver's seat back and bent forward, trying to lower my head between my knees as the panic-induced dizziness threatened to overtake me.

A knock on my passenger window startled me and I screamed. An elderly gentleman was standing beside my car. "Are you okay?" he mouthed.

Not really, but there was nothing he could do to help. I nodded weakly and gave a shaky thumbs up. He hesitated but continued on his way, disappearing around the corner as suddenly as he'd appeared.

I called Nic. "Nicole," I said, my voice hoarse.

"What's up, Beaches?" she said, sassy as always, not realising the seriousness of my situation.

I struggled to gather my thoughts but apparently my heavy breathing and inability to speak were suspicious enough. "Trix? You okay? What's going on?"

"I'm... okay. You know my first claim with the mango?"

"Of course," she said. "What about it?"

"The news on the radio just now... They said that the spider weaver has escaped. Darius...he's...he's been sighted in Kawana Waters. He tried to kill me. I'm scared."

"Fuck," Nic exclaimed. "Fuck. Shit. Fuck. Okay. Nope, this is fine. You're okay. You've got me, you've got Altan. You're a kickass warrior woman who is getting stronger every day. We won't let anything happen to you."

"Or Millie," I breathed. A thought struck me. "She's with Ellie. I need to call her."

"I'll do that. Millie will be fine. We've got this. Call Altan and let him know. We're a team. We'll protect you until that bastard is caught."

"Right. Yes." She had no idea that Altan had just abandoned me. "Thanks, Nic."

"It's okay, babe. Just come home, okay? I'll call Ellie now and get Millie back here."

"Thank you. Love you, Nic."

"Love you too, woman. Now get your ass home."

"I'm coming now," I whispered and hung up.

Staring through my windshield, I wondered how my entire life could change so drastically in twenty-four hours.

A message pinged on my phone. Glancing down, I hoped in vain to see Altan's name on my lockscreen.

It wasn't Altan.

No Caller ID

Hi Trix, long time, no see. It's Darius. We need to talk.

Links

If you enjoyed Gosh Darn Griffins, please leave a review:
https://altippett.com/rl/3938830

Dive into Trix's next adventure with Son of a Spider Weaver, Book Three of the Magic and Motherhood series:
https://altippett.com/rl/4604237

Want to read more books by A. L. Tippett?

Read A Dragon's Mind, Book One in The MINATH Chronicles:
https://altippett.com/rl/3937325

Claim your FREE short story when you subscribe to my monthly newsletter:
https://altippett.com/latest-updates/subscribe/

Get to know me by visiting:
https://altippett.com

Or by following my socials:
https://facebook.com/altippettauthor
https://instagram.com/a_l_tippett_author
https://tiktok.com/@altippettbooks
https://bookbub.com/profile/a-l-tippett
https://goodreads.com/altippett

Acknowledgements

Firstly, I want to say a heartfelt thank you for reading this story. I couldn't do what I do without your support. I hope you loved reading it as much as I loved creating it.

If you enjoyed this book, please consider leaving a review on Amazon, Goodreads, BookBub, or my website. But please remember to be kind. I poured a part of my soul into these pages and, while my brain knows that it won't be everyone's cup of tea (and that's okay), my heart craves acceptance. I'm always happy for readers to email me with constructive feedback.

And don't forget to check out the hijinks in Book Three: *Son of a Spider Weaver*. Poor Trix's world was just turned upside down so make sure you join her as she figures out that all is not as it seems...

I want to sincerely thank the professionals who helped make *Gosh Darn Griffins* the best story that it could be. In particular, thanks to my editor, Karen Holmes, for her kindness, patience, and expertise.

A massive thank you to my cover designer, Ravenborn Covers. I absolutely adore your work.

Thanks also to the artist of my glorious griffin chapter heading art, Urban Rex Designs.

Many thanks to my wonderful alpha and beta readers (and unofficial cheer squad), Claire, Zoe, Kara, and Jen. You ladies are truly wonderful! And a special mention to my mentor, Heather G Harris, for her steadfast support.

A thousand thank yous to all the family members and friends who have continued to support me as I follow my dream.

Last, but not least, thank you to the most important people in my life.

Mum and Dad, life has given you a few knocks recently but you keep getting back up. You are a constant source of inspiration. Thank you for everything. Your unwavering support and love means so much to me. Love you uttmasaba.

To my children, you bring me so much joy. Thank you for inspiring me to be a better person. I love you both beyond words and beyond worlds. I hope I make you proud.

Last, but not least, to the man who made me believe in love again. "Thank you" seems too small a phrase to adequately express my gratitude. You're the reason this book got finished. And more than that, you're the reason I've found my happiness again. I love you, Will.

My heart is full of love and I am so thankful to everyone who has joined me on this wild journey so far. I can't wait for the next adventure.

Fly fierce, strike strong.

April xo

About the Author

I was born in the South Island of New Zealand before my family and I moved to Australia when I was two years old. We lived on a yacht for a few years and travelled along the east coast of Aussie and across the Pacific Ocean to New Caledonia. My parents schooled us via Distance Education while we sailed the seas until we bought a house on the Sunshine Coast in Queensland. I finally got to go to "real-school" and loved it – I couldn't understand why we had weekends (because, apparently, I am, and always will be, a big nerd).

Shortly before beginning high school, we moved north to a rural property near Mackay. The big draw card was that I could finally buy my own horse, a dream I'd had since I was a little girl.

Then, I started writing. I began work on my first fantasy novel when I was twelve but abandoned it after deciding that being an author wasn't a "real" job and therefore not worth pursuing. After completing my secondary schooling, my parents encouraged me to experience the real world before committing to a university degree. So, I applied to be a rider in a travelling horse show! Unfortunately, I wasn't successful so instead I did the complete opposite and got a job as an insurance broker. I worked in insurance for seven years before leaving to start a family.

I am now the mother of two wonderful children. It's tricky finding the time to write with two young kids (whilst combatting sleep deprivation!) but, thankfully, I have a Will in my life now, and he helps me find a way. I can't wait to get started on my next book and am looking forward to sharing many more stories with you!